D0390833

YELLOW SHOE FICTION

Michael Griffith, *Series Editor*

The GREATEST Show

STORIES

Michael Downs

LOUISIANA STATE UNIVERSITY PRESS
BATON ROUGE

Published by Louisiana State University Press
Copyright © 2012 by Michael G. Downs
All rights reserved
Manufactured in the United States of America
LSU Press Paperback Original
First printing

Designer: Laura Roubique Gleason
Typefaces: Minion pro, text; Art Gothic, display
Printer and binder: McNaughton & Gunn

LIBRARY OF CONGRESS CATALOGING-IN-PUBLICATION DATA

Downs, Michael, 1964–
    The greatest show : stories / Michael Downs.
        p. cm.
    ISBN 978-0-8071-4452-7 (pbk. : alk. paper) — ISBN 978-0-8071-4453-4 (epub) —
ISBN 978-0-8071-4454-1 (mobi) — ISBN 978-0-8071-4455-8 (pdf)
    I. Title.
    PS3604.O9524G74 2012
    813'.6—dc23

                                                                    2011037858

The paper in this book meets the guidelines for permanence and durability of the
Committee on Production Guidelines for Book Longevity of the Council on Library
Resources. ∞

Stories in this book originally appeared—sometimes in different forms—as follows:

Georgia Review: "Ania"; *Louisiana Literature:* "Ex-Husband, Years Removed" (as
"Go Forth, Christian Spirit"); *Gettysburg Review:* "Ellen at the End of Summer";
Five Points: "Mrs. Liszak" and "Elephant"; *Alaska Quarterly Review:* "Son of Captain
America"; *Missouri Review:* "At the Beach"; *Oxford Magazine:* "Boxing Snowmen";
New Letters: "The Greatest Show"; *Kenyon Review:* "History Class."

"Elephant" was republished in *High Five: An Anthology of Fiction from Ten Years of
"Five Points"* (Carroll and Graf, 2006). "At the Beach" was republished in *City Sages*
(City Lit Press, 2010).

for Sheri
and for Judy and Ed Downs

If we should weep when clowns put on their show,
If we should stumble when musicians play,
Time will say nothing but I told you so.

—W. H. Auden

Contents

★The★ GREATEST Show

Ania

THEIR COURTSHIP BEGAN IN THE SUMMER OF 1936 WHEN SHE WAS
seventeen and he was twenty. He worked as a logger, and one evening he came from the woods wearing muddy boots and carrying a
basket of common mushrooms he had gathered as a gift for her. His
hands were chapped and shy, but he was strong, and though she did
not believe him when he promised to take her to America, the idea
thrilled her. When winter came Ania and Kazimierz married. Soon
after, they left their Polish village in a loud railcar bound for the Bal-
tic coast, then endured endless days in the cramped depths of steer-
age, and because he had kept his promise, Ania knew Kazimierz loved
her. In that new land, he changed his name to Charlie and found a job
in a typewriter factory; he learned English so he could teach her and
the child she carried. Ania recited after him—"Hello, how are you?"
and "Good-bye!"—and she thought her husband so worthy that she
must love him.

Every morning and every evening, in gratitude, Ania prayed.
She lit penny candles, crossed herself, and gave thanks—for Charlie who worked one shift at the factory and another at a warehouse,
for their new life away from the war just started in Europe, and later
for their boy, Teddy. After each "amen," she kissed her fingertips and
touched them to the face of the icon from home, a black-and-white
picture of the Blessed Mother, the shadow-faced Black Madonna of

Częstochowa. Then Ania would pinch the wicks and slide into bed beside her husband. Some nights, Charlie would caress her forehead and her cheeks with callused hands that smelled of machine oil until she whispered, "No. Sleep now."

Ania kept the picture of the Black Madonna enshrined on a half-moon table in the corner of the bedroom and decorated with ribbons and dried flowers. She dusted the picture and the table every day and sometimes added freshly cut blooms of dandelion or forsythia.

The family attended Mass each Sunday, and it was through the church that Ania met Mrs. Patterson, who had volunteered when the priest announced that a couple from Poland needed help adapting to their new country. Mrs. Patterson, married to a young lawyer, lived in West Hartford on a street where servants used hidden staircases, but she was not much older than Ania, and her casual manner allowed Ania to believe the food, the books, and the spare clothes were gifts, not charity. Mrs. Patterson even hired Ania to clean house, and later arranged for her to work for neighbors until Ania knew every banister, every pane of beveled glass, every marble ashtray on Walbridge Road—knew them so well they bored her. Then, what interested her were the pieces she never cleaned, such as the desk where Mrs. Patterson kept letters, calendars, and newspaper articles. Each time Ania passed the desk, she spied on Mrs. Patterson's life.

And then the Japanese attacked Pearl Harbor; the following summer, Mr. Patterson enlisted. His wife threw a farewell picnic party, paying Ania a few dollars to make food and lemonade. On that muggy August afternoon the guests ran out of ice for their drinks, and Mr. Patterson's father at the horseshoe pit was calling, "Can't we get ice in this country anymore?" Ania searched for another block in the kitchen and in the basement, and finding none, looked instead for Mrs. Patterson.

Dance music swung through the halls from a radio upstairs, and though Ania did not then know Benny Goodman, his "Jersey Bounce" would later remind her of that other noise she had heard as she climbed the Pattersons' staircase, a sound obscured by the band's mellow reeds and snapping brass. Someone crying. No, worse than that. Someone gasping—swallowing whole chunks of grief. Unable to resist, Ania crept to the open door of the bedroom.

On the floor, in sunlight, Mr. Patterson sat holding his wife, her sobs fierce, her fists clenching bunches of his starched uniform, her face pressed against his ribcage. Ania hid, but she could not look away. Something in Mrs. Patterson's grief seemed terrible and pure, something that reminded Ania of only one thing: how on first seeing Teddy, red and squalling, she felt as if she had touched the electric nerve where everything begins and ends, so far from this world it is nearly forgotten.

Ania watched the Pattersons and saw nothing of herself or her husband; this surprised her and made her think of him. She pictured his face—so often surprised, so rarely delighted—and she felt neither the pain nor the love Mrs. Patterson poured into the summer afternoon, but only—and this for the first time—a bloodless pity. Later, after she sneaked away to scrape ketchup from plates, she worried that she had never loved Charlie at all, that she had only agreed to accept his passion because it pleased her, then had mistaken her decision for something more.

The next morning she made pancakes—Charlie's favorite breakfast. She fetched aspirin for his vodka headache and laid a hot cloth on his forehead. When he came home from the factory the following Monday, she unlaced his boots and washed his feet with a soft, warm rag. As days and weeks passed, she worked to be a loving wife, to hide her deceit and atone for it. Nights, after Teddy fell asleep, when Charlie came to her shy and wanting as a teenage boy, she fooled him with false enthusiasm, but that only made him seem a fool. She began to resent him, and though she still made him pancakes, she mixed less sympathy into the batter. She no longer pretended. Wounded and confused, he brought home cut flowers or a pastry from the Italian bakery. Ania could think of nothing to say—there was nothing worth saying—so kept silent, and then Charlie spoke only to Teddy, in English, about baseball and the Yankees, and sometimes when Ania was in the room Charlie told the boy how fortunate he was to have such a beautiful mother. They lived this way for a few months. Then, in December—a year after Pearl Harbor—Charlie quit his two jobs and enlisted.

When he left for induction, a gunnysack over his shoulder, Ania stood in the doorway of their apartment holding Teddy, who played with her dark curls. Charlie cupped the back of Teddy's head with his hand, whispered in the boy's ear. Then he stepped back off the landing, one foot lowered to the first stair, his face docile and sad.

Because it was her duty as his wife and cruel to do otherwise, Ania kissed him quickly on the lips. He seemed startled, hurt; but then he was downstairs, and then he was gone.

Charlie wrote long letters, addressing them to "Dearest Ania and Teddy" and signing them "With affection and love—Papa." He included in each letter a portion of his pay. Ania answered his letters with long ones of her own, each ponderous with detail and empty of affection. But those letters took so long to write, and there was so little time now that he was gone. She gave whole afternoons to standing in lines for meat or for heating oil, and prices had risen, so she cleaned even more houses on Walbridge Road. Her letters grew shorter by a page, then by two, and then her replies became sporadic. His continued, long and intimate, describing wakeful nights with no word spoken louder than a whisper for fear of drawing fire, and daylong marches through parching heat. In one envelope he included a photograph of himself sitting on a rock beside trees that grew small and twisted. "Show this to Teddy, so I am not a stranger later," he wrote.

He continued to send money. When she spent it, Ania felt dirty, like a thief, and then she hated his money but had no choice. Prices rose every day. Even with Charlie's pay, she could barely make the rent. To save pennies she took thread from old clothes to mend others. She sold her ration cards on the black market for a little extra and that way could afford meat for one meal a week. No one chastised her when she failed to drop a coin in the collection plate at Mass, but the looks of pity from other parishioners embarrassed her. She sat with

Teddy farther and farther toward the back of the church until it became habit to arrive late and leave early, and then they did not go at all.

★　★　★

The first time she prayed to the Black Madonna—Our Lady of Częstochowa, Our Most Chaste Queen of Poland—Ania was seven years old and her own mother had just died from fever. They buried Mama in a cemetery near the river that ran through Królik Polski, their village, and a priest came to say the words over her grave. The next day, Papa and Ania folded the church clothes of the two younger children, stuffed them into sacks, and the family started a walk that would last more days than Ania could count. It was autumn: cold and rainy, and the roads out of the foothills were thick with mud; Papa gave each child a turn on his shoulders. When any of them complained, he would say, "I know you miss her, but soon it will be better." Now and again farmers in horse-drawn wagons offered rides, which Papa would accept, though Ania sat to the back to avoid the drivers who stared at her. "Such a pretty mane," they might say. "What beautiful skin." Those who said nothing frightened her the most.

On clear nights, Papa lit cooking fires and the children slept in tall grass or in piles of hay, limbs tangled, dirty fingers in mouths, warm beneath their *pierzyna,* the goose-feather quilt their mother had made. When there were clouds, the family took shelter in barns damp with manure. Ania often thought about her mother and tried to imagine heaven, which frightened her, because she could only picture constant light and summer heat and all the angels wearing the same white robes.

One afternoon, Ania saw in the distance that the road led to a field with a tower at its center, surrounded by leafless trees. Closer, she marveled at the walls that surrounded the tower—walls as tall as the trees, built from rough gray stones each as large as a cattle trough, and with wooden doors three times Papa's height. The clouds broke, and Ania saw how parts of the tower caught the sudden light and juggled it. Only that, and she wondered whether she had been wrong about heaven; if it looked like this tower, that would be all right. She imagined her mother waiting inside.

Papa helped them change into their wrinkled church clothes. Then they passed through the tall doors into a garden where priests walked about, then on to another building—a church. A tower bell rang three times.

Inside the church, Ania heard birds and, looking up, saw them sweep across the radiant faces of men painted on the faraway ceiling. Papa made the children hold hands, and they walked deeper into shadows, past things that glowed and things that shined and past big, light-swallowing things. Ania could name none of it: not the drapes or tapestries, not the wooden pews chipped and polished from hundreds of years of use (prettier than the benches in their small church back home), not the mosaics of saints lit by flickering candles—but all of it seemed a gift.

The littlest cried, and Papa lifted him, bouncing him until he was quiet. They joined a line of people waiting to enter a room. A woman chewed at her lips and bobbed, hands clasped, working beads through her fingers; a one-legged man leaned on a stick, his eyes wet, his beard flecked with crumbs; another man clothed in rags scratched his arms and chest, which were covered in bleeding sores. This was no heaven, after all.

Ania left her father's side to peek into that other room, but with a hiss he called her back. When it came their turn to go in, Papa again warned the children to be quiet. Hat in hand, he squatted beside them as they looked upon a woman painted on a board, her right cheek gashed twice so that wood showed behind the paint, her face blackened by smoke from the constellation of candles before her. Around her head shone a circle of light like a crown, and in her lap a boy with a crown like his mother's waved two fingers at Ania. The woman's nose seemed to Ania too long and her mouth too small to eat anything but berries, and she did not smile, so Ania thought the cuts in her cheek must hurt. Still, the woman's hand beckoned as if there were room in her lap for one more, and Papa touched Ania's back, nudging her forward.

"Children," he said, "Our Lady is your mother now."

★ ★ ★

Crossing Walbridge Road toward the Pattersons' house through the high torch of a July day, Ania could feel the soles of her shoes stick to the asphalt. Her thighs slapped together under her skirt, and her blouse plastered itself to her back. Teddy's small hand sweated in hers. Inside, Ania shouted "Hello" over the roar of the electric fans, and Mrs. Patterson appeared in the entry hall, a gaunt, talcum-powdered ghost clutching a damp handkerchief at her neck where her dress hung open. In the nearly two years since her husband had left, she had lost too much weight, as if grief consumed her from within.

"Ania," she sighed. "Nothing special today. No one will visit in this heat, except maybe Ruth Bartlett, and she's not the sort to notice the top of the icebox."

"I have Teddy."

Mrs. Patterson paused as if considering how best to hide her concern. "You know I love Teddy," she said, and she rubbed the boy's head. "Just keep an eye on him, would you?"

In the kitchen, Ania helped Teddy into a chair at the table. "No moving from this seat, Little Monkey," she said. She lifted his hands in front of his face and shook them. "No touching, either."

He pouted, looking so much like his father, and Ania—sorry for Teddy and a little guilty—let go one of his hands and opened the other, tapping the palm with her finger as a sparrow pecks seed from the grass. Then she tugged at the end of each of his fingers as the mama sparrow fed her little ones, saying, "Temu dała, temu dała, temu dała . . ." and then, at the little finger, the bad chick got none, but instead Mama Sparrow snatched off his head—"Temu nic nie dała"—and flew away, and Ania wiggled her fingers up Teddy's arm to his ticklish neck. He squealed, squeezing her hand between his butter-soft cheek and shoulder.

She swept the entry hall, dusted in the furnace-like heat of the sunroom, and polished the empty space on the buffet where a week before Teddy had broken a vase. Since then, all the Walbridge Road women looked at Teddy with nervous eyes that worried Ania, who could not leave him home, but could not afford to lose any job, either. The landlord had raised the rent again, threatening eviction if Ania did not pay, and everything cost so much . . .

She rested on a footstool near Mrs. Patterson's desk in the study, pulling her skirt's hem high over her knees and taking deep breaths. She leaned near the desk, looking for a magazine to use as a hand fan, but there was none, only a train timetable, a letter from Maine, a blue-penciled note on the calendar: "Junior League @ 7 p.m.—circus tickets to orphans." On the blotter, tied with string, was the stack: two dozen or more, each stiffer than a playing card and printed with the words "Ringling Bros. and Barnum and Bailey Combined Shows (Good afternoon only July 6)." Ania touched them, wondering why Mrs. Patterson hadn't offered tickets to her. She had never seen a circus. Teddy had never seen one, either. But how could she expect anything when Mrs. Patterson had already given clothes and food and money, when Teddy had broken the vase?

Fast as she could, Ania fluffed the study's curtains and retied them, remembering Teddy trapped in the chair. She swept a spider's web from beside a bookcase, then peeked at the circus tickets again, wondering how long she and Teddy could last through the heat and work of summer, heat and work and heat and work and her little boy never to leave his chair. What difference would one day make, one day away? She climbed the servant staircase to change Mrs. Patterson's bed, to shake sheets that billowed weightless as air, to wipe a hot iron over lacy pillowcases.

Then, with chores complete and sweat stinging her eyes, she

sneaked back to the desk, slipped two tickets from the bundle, and hid them in the waistband of her skirt.

Before bedtime, Ania set the circus tickets on her dresser among a clutter of hairpins, buttons, and unread letters from Charlie, then knelt before the Black Madonna. With candle flames undisturbed, with the neighborhood noises of boys roughhousing, screen doors slamming, dogs barking to scare the world, Ania tried to explain why she took the tickets, how she so wanted Teddy to spend a day laughing, his eyes opened to a place beyond his imagining in the way her eyes had been opened the day she and Charlie arrived in America.

"For the sake of the boy," she prayed, "bless my sin."

Teddy appeared then at her door, his cheeks flushed and eyes struggling against sleep not quite broken. "I had a nightmare," he said. He crawled onto the mattress, and Ania blew out the candles. She bunched the sheet at the foot of the bed because it was too stifling even for that, then lay beside her boy. She held him as she would a doll, felt him expand with each whistling breath, and she knew that anything done for him was, yes, for the good.

Though Ania had never seen a circus, a carnival had passed through Królik Polski after each Easter, and the performers sometimes roomed with families. One year, following a difficult winter, Papa rented the children's room to a snake charmer. The man wore a glass-bead necklace and bracelets that rattled, and his skin looked gray as spent ashes. Ania pretended to mind her chores when he was around, but all the while watched him—how he walked with a hop, how he smoothed his eyebrows with fingers dampened by the tip of his tongue—and as she listened to him sing to his serpents in some alien language, something in her grew giddy at his strangeness. When the carnival left the village, he sneaked away, leaving for his room and board only a snakeskin tacked to the wall over Ania's bed. Papa wanted to burn it, but Ania begged to keep it. That day, and for years after, she would lose herself in the patterns of the skin.

The morning of the circus was hot and damp; the afternoon worse. Teddy led her by the hand along crowded Barbour Street, past vendors selling orange slices, past accordion players, tumblers, and jugglers— Teddy tugging because she never walked fast enough—and finally to the circus grounds, where one enormous tent rose amidst smaller tents and railroad cars. A red-faced man in a lime-colored coat waved people forward, promising "Mysteries, Magic, and Amazement! The Greatest Gathering since the Heavenly Host!" and Ania thought he looked beautiful, and she believed him.

Dizzy with faces and sounds, she pulled Teddy to her and pushed toward the big top, inhaling the musky air, welcoming the jumble of color, amazed at the pictures painted on boards that showed how men could swallow fire, how women could grow beards, how boys Teddy's age could live joined at the hip. Teddy pointed at a clown—"Look!"— and at a pony—"Look!"—and each time Ania looked not with her own eyes but with his, sharing his awe.

At the big-top entrance, while she and Teddy waited to show their tickets, Ania noticed a clown, sitting away from the crowd on a trunk, nearly hidden by a fold in the tent. The clown had placed his hat and a frizzy yellow wig in his lap, and he cupped a cigarette in his hand, pinching it between his forefinger and thumb, its long ash drooping. Elbows on knees, he patted his brow with a handkerchief, then looked at the damp spot on the cloth. Ania thought of Charlie home from work, in his rocking chair, his hat on the table beside it, forehead pink where the hatband had pressed.

The clown raised his face, noticed her. Past the painted grin, past the white face that ended at his thin hair, Ania saw in his eyes the same look Charlie had brought home from the factory each evening, the same vacant weariness she saw in the mirror after a day spent on Walbridge Road. A line of sweat slid the length of the clown's cheek, and Ania recalled soiled bathrooms in expensive houses and fine dust settled on crystal bowls. The circus music became noise. The air stank with animal droppings. She offered her tickets to a man who tore them, mumbling, "Grandstand, ma'am."

Teddy begged for peanuts, so they stopped at a vendor who scooped a bagful from a barrel drum that spun over a coal fire. Then Teddy led Ania to folding chairs near the top of the crowded grandstand, so high they could almost touch the sagging canvas above. She held Teddy's hand, warm as a biscuit from the oven, then wrapped her arms around him. He felt so small, so easy to surround and swallow into her body. She rested her chin on the delicate bone of his shoulder so they touched cheek to soft cheek, and she smelled the tang of his skin.

A man wearing a red coat and a black stovepipe hat leapt into the center ring. "Ladies and Gentlemen!" he yelled into a megaphone. "Children of all ages! Welcome to the big top! Welcome to the Ringling Brothers and Barnum and Bailey Circus!"

A brass band played a rump-de-diddly fanfare while horses, clowns, and dogs filled the rings. Ania's hands fell lightly on Teddy's shoulders and she watched, surprised, as the light in his face disappeared, replaced by fear. It seemed too much for him, all at once.

Then the rings emptied—animals scampering back to their cages, clowns disappearing in folds of the tent—and trapeze artists appeared on platforms high above the rings. Teddy turned in her lap to hide his face in her side. Ania recognized a song the band played: "Stars and Stripes Forever."

At that moment, a flash of orange appeared on the other side of the big top, then rose up the wall of the tent. Ania thought it must be part of the performance, it seemed such a miraculous thing. But the crowd fell quiet, and then a thunder rumbled from all around and someone yelled "Fire!" and the thunder exploded, flames charging up and across the billowing roof of the tent, people rushing from the bleachers, knocking chairs underfoot. A trapeze artist jumped from his platform, and Ania watched him twist through air to the sudden ground. She grabbed Teddy and chased the crowd, but at the bottom of the bleachers her foot twisted in a chair and she fell, her face scraping dirt, Teddy tumbling beneath her. Someone stepped on her; her ribs cracked, her breath shot away. "Mama!" Teddy cried, but heat struck the back of Ania's neck and she curled into a ball, screaming in answer to the screams in her ears, kicking her legs as people trampled them. "Let me up!" she shouted as she sucked and coughed black smoke. The heat wrapped round her, wave after wave sinking deeper until it was underneath her skin and invading her muscles and bone. She managed to stand, but with knifing pain her legs gave way and she fell again. Teddy, in a tantrum, his distorted face unfamiliar through soot and fear, slapped at the ground now strewn with peanuts from the empty bag he yet gripped with a tiny fist. Overhead, flames crept from the blackness like sluggish lightning. Fire rained as a flap of the tent collapsed, swatches of fiery canvas falling on the scrambling crowd and the panicked animals snarling and chattering in cages. A tent pole crashed near Ania, and flaming ropes lashed her face and legs. She beat her arms against her burning skirt as a boy tumbled past, his shirt gone except the buttoned cuffs, the skin of his arms and chest turned black and puddled, and Ania reached for him, but the boy was too fast. And now even the ground burned, and bodies red and black writhed among the fractured chairs. "Mother!" Ania wailed to heaven, praying and cursing in two languages, defying everything, "Mother!" She wrapped her arms around Teddy and, though the muscles of her legs ripped with each step, she limped first one way and then another, forward then back, the heat so massive she couldn't breathe, her arms tingling as hair evaporated and skin blistered, a stink in the air worse than any she had known.

And then she stopped. She stopped.

Above her in the flames she saw a haloed face, shimmering through the smoke, and Ania squinted against the ash dust in her eyes to see more clearly the two scars, the placid mouth, the wide-set and beatific eyes of the Black Madonna. Teddy wailed, but she heard him only at a great distance, his noise baffled by another sound that glided through her—a rising, resonating chime. Ania closed her eyes, touched her dry tongue to her lips. When she looked again through tears, all her panic disappeared, and in its place Ania felt overcome by an exhilarating serenity, and she stepped toward the face, forward into the flames, reaching out to the hellish sky.

Ania floated in warmth as if in a pond of summer water, or maybe in the air, her heart marking a gentle rhythm as she breathed the sweetness of wildflowers, and then it was gone, only a memory of pleasure that receded as if the thing remembered never was. In its place, Ania had the sense that patches of her skin were peeled away, raw and naked and hot, and thirst emptied her throat of anything but the need for water. She gasped, and the air she breathed seemed barely enough, but each breath—no matter how slight—racked her from bone to flesh. Her heart raced. From all sides she heard groans and shrieks and shouts, and she smelled an odor like rotting bark and then the stench of something burned, and she knew that stench came from her.

She cried Teddy's name.

A masked nurse with gloved hands forced her back down on the hospital bed. Half of Ania's face hurt beyond screaming, and her right hand did, too, and her legs throbbed, and she shivered but could think only about Teddy and the fire and his face marked with ash and smoke and clean lines where tears had washed the skin. Where was her boy? Was he all right? Was he alive?

How long this lasted she never could recall. In years to come, she remembered only her fear, a commotion, hands everywhere, faces masked except for their frightened eyes, voices shouting, everything white and shiny, and she remembered, too, a need to have Teddy curled beside her, and then a whisper at her ear that Teddy was alive and that a doctor would explain everything. After that, only the pain bothered her.

But all that day, no doctor spoke of Teddy. Though she pleaded to see him, the nurses said no, she couldn't leave her bed and neither could he. When a nurse came to cut and peel and scrub away the dead skin around her face and on her hand, Ania asked again. She whimpered his name even as the skin came away, exposing patches of pink nerves that bolted at the touch of air so that other nurses had to hold Ania's kicking legs and flailing arms. A nurse shaved Ania's head, and another smeared cream on Ania's face, then covered her right eye with bandages. A few hours later, when those bandages came off, Ania screamed curses in Polish and in English because her deep, dead skin came off with them.

When the nurses and doctors left her alone to rest, when the pain, though never gone, rested too, she worked to understand the pleasure she had felt, the singing joy of body and soul that began in the fury of the tent when she had looked up and seen the scarred, sooted face of her Blessed Mother. But she could recall only a dim picture, and the sensations remained impossible to re-create. She remembered stumbling forward—Teddy in her arms—toward that face, toward the fire, too. Others had passed her, hurrying the other way, but she headed deeper into the tent, past empty cages and burning chairs and an up-ended peanut cart. Now, amidst other patients who cried and moaned, the cruelty of the tent seemed the thing most real, and she wondered whether she had been delivered or betrayed.

"Ania?" Mrs. Patterson said, and Ania awoke, ending a dream of Mass in the small church back home; Father Petrykowski's face had been painted like a clown's, and he had refused her the Host, holding a lit candle to her lips instead.

Mrs. Patterson wore a surgical mask, and her hands were gloved; a moment passed before Ania recognized the eyes, before she realized they belonged not to a nurse come to cause pain but to someone else. For the first time in days Ania felt relief, but that lasted no longer than a breath, because she remembered her theft and what had come of it.

"Don't cry, Ania. Everything's all right now."

Ania listened to that early-morning voice full of promise and light, and she wanted to confess to her, relieve the guilt, but who then would be left to visit her when Mrs. Patterson, betrayed and disgusted, walked away?

"I brought Teddy into the fire." Ania's voice broke, and she clutched the collar of her paper-thin gown. "The nurses still won't let me see him. Bacteria, they say. He's my son, I say. But they're hard-hearted."

"Oh, I know. The weeks can seem forever, but you'll see him soon. I know you will."

With a finger from her good hand Ania traced circles on the bedsheet, the circles becoming an oval, the oval becoming a face, and Ania added two straight lines as scars. "Teddy and I, we send messages through a priest," Ania said. "He writes them for us, carries them back and forth."

"I'll visit Teddy, too. I'll tell him that you miss him." Mrs. Patterson pointed at the burn on Ania's face. "That looks like it's healing," she said. "Here. I brought some things from your apartment. Clothes for when you leave, some mail. There's a cablegram from Charlie." She held up an envelope.

Ania shivered. "Will you take off your mask?" she said. "I have to see a face."

"They told me not to," Mrs. Patterson said, but then she reached behind her head and unknotted the strings. The mask fell around her neck, and with obvious effort Mrs. Patterson smiled, her lips daubed rose, a copper shadow over her eyes and rouge on her cheeks, her brown hair rolled into a bun that leaned down the back of her neck. It seemed to Ania a perfect face, a face Mr. Patterson must miss.

"Shall I read the cable from Charlie? I can leave it for you to open later."

He would blame her. Ania imagined words of anger and accusation, how she had hurt him. Though afraid, she said, "Please."

Mrs. Patterson tugged the envelope open and unfolded the tissue-thin paper. "Good news," she said. "The army's granted him emergency leave. He's coming home."

★ ★ ★

He walked in on Sunday afternoon a week later, dressed in a starched uniform, a khaki-colored necktie tucked inside his shirt above the chest button, a double-stripe chevron on each sleeve. His hair was trimmed short, and he wore a surgical mask. One gloved hand held his cap, folded flat; in the other he carried a box wrapped in silver paper and red ribbon. When he sat beside her, he set the box on the floor and reached toward her elbow.

"The nurses say no," she said.

He pulled his hand away. His eyes softened as if distressed by how she had changed, and it was only then she knew how badly her face must be burned. The nurses, the doctors, the priest—none had brought her a mirror.

"I wish I had been there," he said, and she heard in his voice that he relived the fire, too, imagined her there, her and Teddy, and she felt embarrassed by his weakness: She deserved scorn, not sympathy. Ania turned her face away. Three beds down, a doctor and nurses worked on another survivor whose moans sometimes rose into screams.

"They wouldn't let me bring flowers," he said. She heard him unwrap the package, the tape snapping, the paper crumpling. "It's a picture," he said.

She looked and saw the three of them together: Teddy, an infant in his christening gown, on her lap; Charlie with his arm around the back of her chair. Ania had insisted on sending a print to her father in Poland, though Charlie told her the Germans controlled everything and would never deliver it. Charlie, always so practical.

He set the happy family on her bedside.

She knew why he had brought the portrait, and she feared a reunion would create a household even worse than what they had shared before; it was worse now for his kindness. More than ever, she wanted the flames and the punishment, wanted the heat to burn away her shame, her guilt, her remorse, leave all of it ashes and her, too, if purging the rest required it. Perhaps she was meant for the fire; perhaps that had been why Our Lady appeared in the smoke. *She* was a mother, after all, and didn't all mothers understand that miracles— even the forgiveness of Ania's sins—required pain and suffering? Ania had escaped the fire too soon. A mistake. For if she had remained in the presence of the Black Madonna, all that was wrong and sinful would have been engulfed, purified, erased in the passion, and Ania would lie now in her hospital bed bathed in grace.

"You can't come home," she said to Charlie. "You left. You left."

His face—the parts she could see—changed: the eyes widened, the ears reddened. "You can't come home," she said again. "And you can't have Teddy. You can't . . ."

When Charlie walked out, he took the photograph.

On the day Ania left the hospital, the nurses gave her permission to visit Teddy. They made her wear a white gown over her clothes, as if she were still a patient, and a white mask over her face. She changed in a lavatory. A month had passed since the fire, and for the first time she saw her scar, the skin raised in a purple patch over the right half of her forehead, along her scalp, covering her right eye, ending in a line that ran across her cheekbone to her ear. With her good hand, she touched the rubbery new flesh that intrigued and horrified her. To cover her shaved head, Ania tied a brilliant blue scarf the nurses gave her as a farewell.

He lay with other boys in a room made for them, the walls painted blue and all the beds small. Teddy's bed, with bars around it, made Ania think of the cages around the circus rings. But wires and tubes snaked into this cage, and in the midst of it her baby lay swaddled in white sheets.

A nurse lowered the bars on one side, and Ania sat in a chair beside the bed. Looking at Teddy frightened her, even more because he was asleep. Wrapped in gauze, forehead sweaty and head shaved bald—Teddy looked less like her boy than some mistake the doctors made while building a child from scratch. Tubes ran to his foot and his groin. The skin on his face, the only skin that had been spared, had lost its softness. His arms and legs were tied with cloth strips to the bars, so he was spread like a bird over the sheets.

"He'll scratch his burns," the nurse said. "Even with his toes if he can reach. If he does that, the grafts might not take, or the infections might get worse."

Ania asked to touch him, but the nurse shook her head.

"Teddy," Ania whispered, "it's Mama."

He opened his eyes, but she could tell he didn't recognize her. Not with the mask.

"I'm hot," he said.

Ania's hands began to shake, and she held them near her mouth. She began to feel hot, too, breathing into the cotton mask.

"It's Mama," she repeated. "It's Mama."

A little before six that evening they made her leave him. Outside Teddy's room, Ania took off the mask and gown and adjusted her blouse, one that was a Christmas gift from Charlie a few years back. She thought of that morning, of Charlie's generosity, as she rode the bus home. There, she saw that he had earlier come for his things, stayed a night or two, then left not to return. He had eaten in the kitchen and washed his plate, fork, and knife and set them in the dish rack. She could tell he had slept in their bed, because the sheets were pulled and tucked tighter than she had ever managed. He had taken clothes from the closet and a pillow from the sofa, and her favorite of Teddy's picture books, about a dog that runs away from home. Also, Ania's hairbrush was missing.

The landlord, fearing German bombs, had painted all the building's window glass black. Ania kept the windows shut, living in shadow, listening in anger to the neighborhood's sounds: hide-and-seek, kick the can, stickball; a cat in heat; a fruit peddler calling out "Peaches!" Afternoons, she visited Teddy. Always she took care to leave him before supper because the nurses told her that was when Charlie stopped by, and Ania feared seeing her husband, though she thought of him often. She imagined him in a two-room apartment somewhere in the city, eating bread and cheese for dinner. She remembered the photograph of the christening, his arm around her back, and tried to remember how it felt—his touch. She came to regret the emptiness of the apartment, especially during the silent, wakeful nights when she lay in bed and relived what they had called the greatest show on earth, saw again the smiling, painted faces of the clowns who, armed with water buckets, shouted and waved, forever laughing at the flames.

On a Wednesday afternoon two weeks after Ania left the hospital, she heard a car pull to the curb, then listened to its engine shut down and the parking brake grind. She didn't leave the couch, not even when the hinges on the downstairs door creaked. No voices, but they were women—Ania could hear high heels clicking at the bottom of the stairwell. She reached for her scarf and opened the door before they could knock. The women fluttered at first like chickadees, their long eyelashes batting, their heads twitching this direction then that—except for Mrs. Patterson, who stood near the back looking at the floor as if she had just misplaced an earring.

Mrs. Griswold, Mrs. Mawson, Mrs. Bartlett, Mrs. Thompson— the women from Walbridge Road. The brightness of their summer dresses and of the white beads on their purses lit the hallway so that its wood looked poorer, its floor dustier, its wallpaper dirtier. Mrs. Griswold, at the front, offered Ania her hand, rainbow-colored bracelets bunched at her plump wrist.

"We're oh so sorry," she said.

Ania invited the women in. All passed her quickly and sat—except Mrs. Patterson, who stopped to lay a gentle, cold hand on Ania's elbow, and whose mouth grew smaller with concern until her red lips formed a carnation.

Ania found another chair for Mrs. Patterson, then switched on a lamp. She fetched ashtrays for Mrs. Mawson and Mrs. Griswold, offered coffee or lemonade and apologized that there was no food. The women assured her that having refreshments for guests should be the last thing on her mind, that it was presumptuous of them, really, to drop in unannounced—and then the women fell silent. They drank and smoked as if they had done something wrong or were witness to something they ought not see. Ania leaned against a radiator near a window, adjusting her robe to cover more, to hide. Their timidity made her nervous.

"Dear," said Mrs. Griswold, "how is your Tommy?"

Mrs. Patterson whispered, "It's Teddy, Katherine."

Ania smiled. He came to her, not as a picture, but as a memory of touch. She could feel him in her arms, his slender hand nesting in hers, his weight in her lap, his body growing breath by breath.

"Some days he is better. Others, he is not."

"Such a dreadful day that was," said Mrs. Thompson. "So many died."

"All those children," said Mrs. Patterson, softly.

"You're fortunate, Ania, you really are," said Mrs. Griswold. "It's a blessing you and Teddy survived."

Ania rubbed her hands together, the left caressing the scar on the right, and tried not to smile. Such a silly woman, Mrs. Griswold. No one in the tent was blessed, except maybe the dead.

When the women declined more lemonade, Ania collected the glasses, each stained with lipstick. "I'll help," Mrs. Patterson said, though Ania had all the glasses in hand. The other women remained behind, not speaking.

In the kitchen, Mrs. Patterson stood next to the sink basin. Her eyes, shadowed blue, shone from her face with such intensity that Ania wanted to look away but couldn't. "There's a check in my pocketbook," Mrs. Patterson said. "It's pay for the month and a half that you've missed, as well as pay for one month more."

"Your homes must need cleaning."

"There's a nice Hungarian woman," Mrs. Patterson said, watching as Ania rinsed the glasses. "She has four boys—older—and all live at home. She does good work. It will be difficult to let her go. But we've decided—all of us—when you want to come back, Ania, the jobs are yours. Of course."

Ania thanked Mrs. Patterson, then laughed without meaning to, without knowing why, and said, "I stole the circus tickets from your desk."

"Oh, dear, I know!" Mrs. Patterson said, panic in her eyes. "I should have given them to you. There you were, with poor Teddy, in my house, like a member of the family, and I didn't even think to . . . and that night, when I counted the tickets—then I heard about the fire. Oh, Ania, I was so afraid."

Mrs. Patterson tinkered with the clasp on her purse, her hands shaking and the clasp resisting her. She pulled a kerchief from her sleeve and dabbed her eyes, which had been stained by leaking mascara. "If you need a loan—anything, really—of course you can ask me," she said. "Ask me for anything. Oh, I hate this."

When the two left the kitchen, the other women already stood by the door, and on the coffee table sat a small of collection of checks. Mrs. Patterson finally managed the clasp of her purse, pulled out her check, and set it atop the rest. Mrs. Griswold sniffed and touched a kerchief to her nose. Mrs. Thompson stood at the door with her hand on the knob.

Mrs. Patterson looked down before offering a hand to Ania, reaching toward the hand without scars.

"You telephone if you need anything," she said. "Anything at all."

As Ania closed the door on the women, as their automobile choked to life, she remembered Mrs. Patterson's touch, its mercy, its selflessness, its insufficiency. She wandered past Teddy's room, the bedcovers neat, the sheets unchanged for so long; and then to the bedroom where she slept alone, and she paused before the half-moon table, its candles filmed with dust, the icon still beckoning. Ania turned from it, wrapped her arms around herself and squeezed. She felt nothing. But her flesh was healed; her skin longed once more for contact, for sensation, for texture, for a warmth that would not burn.

★ ★ ★

"An astringent," said Mrs. Patterson, wiping a cotton ball over Ania's face. "I'm not certain what the word means, but it shuts your pores and cleans your skin." Mrs. Patterson pressed hard with the cotton, and Ania's skin stung in some spots and in others lit up as if touched by a breeze.

Ania sat sideways to her bathroom mirror in a stiff wood chair. Mrs. Patterson stood in front of her, now patting Ania's cheek with two warm fingers, spreading a liquid that felt dry and seemed to stretch Ania's skin, touching everywhere but the scar.

"And this is foundation. I almost can't believe nobody's ever done this for you. I suppose that pretty as you"—Mrs. Patterson took a breath—"pretty as you are, I suppose there never was much reason. But we can always . . . well. There's always a first time, and I'm glad you asked. It surprised me, I have to say, to hear from you so soon. But I'm glad."

Ania turned her face to the mirror for a better look.

"Nothing's happening," she said.

"Not yet. We haven't even started your eyes. That's where you'll notice the difference. Tilt your head back." Mrs. Patterson pressed gentle fingertips to Ania's forehead, spread makeup under Ania's eyes "to get rid of this purple that comes out when you're tired. You do look tired, dear."

Her hands floated around Ania's face, passing under her nose with the scent of bar soap, fingers skipping, palms cupping the side of Ania's head as Mrs. Patterson drew lines on the lids of Ania's eyes, whispering as she worked. . . *Smudge here. That's good. Make you Cleopatra. Charlie will like this, I think. Don't move. This might sting. There. Rouge off the cheekbone. Oops. I'll wipe that. Try again. Yes. Open those eyes. Open. Open. Now powder. Smells like roses, doesn't it? Just a touch. There. Takes the shine off. There. There.*

Mrs. Patterson's fingers working on her, working for her, made gooseflesh of the skin on Ania's arms. Mrs. Patterson's fingers prodding, wiping, dabbing, sweeping, brushing . . .

Her eyes. Facing the mirror, Ania could not stop looking at her own eyes. The rest—her cheekbones, her nose and its bridge, her forehead and chin, her lips—all now subdued by the radiance of her eyes. Even the scar—she remembered the scar and looked at it, but no, Mrs. Patterson made even that less important than the little miracles of her eyes.

"How does it feel?"

"Feel?" said Ania, who had only seen. But now she realized her face felt covered in something inflexible or protective, as if Mrs. Patterson had painted her with some magic salve that could resist even flame.

"It feels hard."

"You'll get used to it." Mrs. Patterson picked through the pouch she'd brought. "Let's not forget the lipstick."

★ ★ ★

Ania waited in the hospital hallway, watching the boy and his father, neither of whom had yet noticed her. Charlie sat, still in uniform, leaning forward with elbows on knees, rubbing his palms together, telling Teddy about a pitcher with the Yankees, who was Polish. She hesitated at the doorway to listen and to watch, standing unsteadily in high heels borrowed from Mrs. Patterson, fiddling with the buttons of a linen dress that Mrs. Patterson had lent her, too. She studied Charlie's hands, how sometimes he raised them in surrender, or made a fist, and once he snapped his fingers. His hands looked clean and vital, so different than when their creases and lines were drawn with grease from the machines he fixed at the factory. She stepped into the room.

Teddy saw her first. His face changed and his mouth fell open. Noticing that, his father turned. Charlie's face paled.

"Mama," Teddy said, and she could see by his frown, by the fear in his eyes, that he thought something was wrong, that having both Mama and Papa at his bedside meant something terrible.

"No, Teddy," she said, rushing to him. "Everything's fine, Little Monkey."

"The nurses say not to touch," Charlie said.

But she had waited too long already—more than two months of the longest days. Ania began to tug at Teddy's fingertips. "Temu dała, temu dała . . . " and at the thumb, "Temu nic nie dała," and she ran her fingers up to his chin, and Teddy giggled and twisted away from her and toward her.

She let go and faced Charlie. "The nurses will clean him," she said.

But Charlie seemed already to have forgotten his warning. He gazed at her, and she saw he was startled by how she looked: not shaved or wounded, not bandaged or shamed.

She tilted her head, as if to study the bag dripping clear liquid into Teddy's toe, but really so that Charlie could better see the scars in the midst of the powder and cream and color. "We're waiting for you," she said to Teddy. "Mama and Papa are waiting for you to come home to us. You come home," she said, "to us." And she reached for Charlie's hand. She reached with the hand that had been burned so that he could feel the lines there, the raised skin, the smooth, waxen flesh.

She pulled Charlie's hand to her face, opened his fingers and let his palm fall on her marred cheek. His ears reddened, making his poor complexion even paler, and she watched his eyes as he examined her the way he might look at a broken engine.

Teddy squirmed in his bed. "I don't want to be tied," he complained, but Ania only said, "I'm sorry, Little Monkey. All the rules we can't break."

Charlie pulled his hand away, and she turned to him, suddenly afraid, but he didn't leave. He took her by the shoulders and guided her into his large lap, where he wrapped his arms tight around her. She tensed at first, letting him squeeze, and she thought of herself as a dishrag in his hands, twisted until all the pain and fear drained, and then her body loosened and his grip did, too, but he didn't let go.

He didn't let go. Settled there in the midst of him, the rhythm of her breath matching his, she thought maybe this was love. She hoped so.

★ ★ ★

At the door of their apartment, she handed Charlie the key. Inside, she patted his rocking chair. "Sit here," she said, then brought him a bottle of beer from the icebox and apologized that there was no vodka.

"There was no vodka overseas, either," he said. "Some bourbon. Mostly beer, though never this cold."

As she cooked dinner she spied on him now and then, but if his gaze turned her way she snapped her attention back to whatever lay before her. Sometimes when she looked up, she caught him looking at her, but he said nothing, and that unnerved her.

Over black bread and pierogi, he asked, "Does it hurt?"

"No," she said. "And the doctors say that after a few years, it will still be purple but not so rough."

"I wish you had written about the money. I always kept a little, but I didn't need it."

"You sent enough." She served him more pierogi. "We survived."

With that last word she flinched; for Teddy the doctors promised nothing. And when she looked across the table at Charlie, who fixed his attention on his plate, she knew he suffered from the same uncertainty.

She washed dishes in the fading light of a late summer sun, handling each plate and each utensil with tenderness, the warm rinse water flowing from the tap without sound, peeling the soap from a plate, then a bowl, then a spoon. Finished, she shook the water from her hands, wiped them in a threadbare towel, then came to him in his chair, leaned over its back, and kissed the lobe of his ear. He stiffened, gripped the arms of the rocking chair so hard that the blue veins rose across the backs of his hands, and she grazed his hand with her fingertips. Tight skin. Callused. Coarse, curled black hair. She dragged her fingertips to his wrist, then stepped away and into their bedroom. With the light off, she began to undress, beginning with the blue scarf. When she heard him behind her, she said in Polish, "Leave the light off." She was afraid for what he would see of her, the hair nubby and not grown back, the scars that in the bedroom she could not show off to him so proudly as she had in the hospital. Here her disfigurement would mark her as a woman different from the Ania he had known before. She needed to be the same, the Ania he loved, the one for whom he would stay. His shoes clumped to the floor behind her, and she heard his belt unbuckle.

When she turned to face him, the window and its pale light behind her, she saw in his jittering eyes, in the way he bit his lip, let it go, bit it again, that he was fearful, and she realized how much joy she still gave him and, yes, how much he loved her. So she stood straight, raised her arms, and welcomed her husband home, troubled and relieved by how much his happiness depended on her.

His lovemaking was familiar and quick, and she knew he had been faithful. Once finished, he whispered, "I love you, I missed you," hand yet clasped to hers, before he fell asleep. With the thumb of that held hand she rubbed Charlie's skin, the same spot over and over. She had hoped for more, for something electric with mystery, yet now she felt nothing but Charlie's skin and, maybe, some gratitude for his weight in the bed, and then a growing unease that all nights would be like this night, that she would forever feel nothing more than skin and gratitude.

Charlie snored, desperately snatching at gulps of breath. The moon no longer shone through the open window. Clammy in the heat, Ania shifted her legs away from her husband and let go his hand. Through the window she heard a baby cry. The sound scared her, or maybe she had been afraid ever since Charlie stepped into the apartment, hinting at the old, quiet order of things from which so much, still, was missing. But it would have to do, there being nothing else.

Ex-Husband, Years Removed

HIS EX-WIFE'S BODY HAD RESTED ONLY A FEW HOURS IN THE CON-
secrated ground, a mound of loose dirt above her and no stone yet to
mark her place. In an ill-furnished apartment on the edge of Hartford's Italian ghetto, Galahad Simmons sat at a card table with the
brother of his ex, the two of them eating celery sticks and drinking
beer from bottles. From where they sat they could hear Gal's sister
drying and storing dishes now that the general mourners had all left.
Gal tapped the table with the corner of an envelope torn open by a finger and marked with the return address of an attorney.

Sweat soaked both men's shirts. The apartment had good light but
no breeze, though every window hung open. A neighbor's radio announced that early reports of two hundred dead appeared to be high.
Latest counts tallied one hundred sixty. "Scores" was how Gal had first
heard the number.

The brother said, "It's vulgar to sue over this."

"It's vulgar to die," said Gal. He pushed the attorney's letter across
the table and thumped it twice with an index finger. "But Sophie did
die. For Christ's sake, think this through. You could buy a house."

"I've heard you. I know what you're saying." He began to mimic
Gal, his words tumbling faster from his mouth, his voice rising an oc-
tave. "*It's how things work, Nick. It's justice, Nick.*"

Gal raised his eyebrows, put forth his hands as if they held gifts.

He said, "There you go. The circus people messed up. That tent never should have burned. So now lawyers sniff a buck. You can't stop them. The money will be there. If you don't take it, somebody else will." Gal pried open another bottle, relaxed with its sigh, then offered the church key to Nick.

"Still working on mine," said Nick. Then: "I'm done with this talk. Give me a poem, huh? She liked how you knew so many poems."

The beer tasted bright. Gal placed the cold bottle against his forehead, closed his eyes. He let his mind leave the room and find a place in memory that harbored lines of verse and his ex-wife. "Nah," he said, "that was a joke with us. I'd recite some moldy sap, ham it up some. She thought it was a stitch."

"You're wrong. She liked it. She said it was beautiful how you spoke."

Gal, who had been passing his walking cane nervously from hand to hand, missed a catch and the cane clattered to the floorboards. He studied the cane, his eyebrows bunching. "Did she?" he said.

"She did."

Now the neighbor's radio reported war news, Allied forces giving the Japs what for in Saipan. In the steamy heat of the apartment the air felt unbreathable. In the circus tent, in Sophie's last moments, the air itself ignited. Gal had heard that awful fact from a rewrite guy in the newsroom. In a picture in his head Sophie sucked fire into her lungs, but she did it with a leering smile, and that image, though he knew it to be false, distressed him. Gal doffed his eyeglasses and cleaned sweat from the lenses with his handkerchief, then wiped his face from temple to temple. "The heat looks better on you than me, I'll wager," Gal said. "Sweat always looks sharp on a boxer. She liked guys with your look, hair wavy and thick, shoulders like a mastodon's. She'd go for that broken nose of yours, too. If you weren't her brother." Nick smiled, a shy grin, compelled more than enjoyed. Gal said, "When do you fight next?"

"Is this for your column?"

"No. Just talk."

"I don't think it matters."

"Nick, it's small talk. C'mon."

Nick struck the butt of his bottle against the tabletop. "Just give me a poem, why don't you?"

Gal clapped his hands once, rubbed the palms together. In the kitchen Lena hummed a vague melody, her voice gentle and clean as a bicycle bell. "Poem. Fine," said Gal. What came to him first were lines from Tennyson, from a memorial poem that would make Sophie guffaw. He pushed away from the table and stood, breathed deeply and coughed to clear his throat. "Alfred, Lord Tennyson," he began. "Two quatrains from 'In Memoriam A. H. H.'"

> *My love involves the love before;*
> *My love is vaster passion now;*
> *Though mixed with God and Nature thou,*
> *I seem to love thee more and more.*
>
> *Far off thou art, but ever nigh;*
> *I have thee still, and I rejoice;*
> *I prosper, circled with thy voice;*
> *I shall not lose thee though I die.*

Nick nodded his approval. "We'll always have her," he said.

Gal lifted his cane from the floor, flicked away a swirl of dust that stuck to the stump-end where the cane's wood had worn round and slivered. He edged his way around the table and squeezed Nick's shoulder. "Some of us lost her long ago," he said. Shuffling off to the kitchen, he glanced away from something he'd noticed when he first came in: a wall poster tacked over a crack, hung crooked, lower on the right. Nick worked first shift on an assembly line building airplane engines, and the poster came from the factory, one of many efforts to encourage patriotism and munitions work, the twain, these days, being one. "You knock 'em out," said the pilot on the poster, giving a thumbs-up from his cockpit. "We'll knock 'em down."

Lena stood from a squat, shutting a low-cabinet door. "This

kitchen needs me," she said. "You don't want to know what I've seen. How's Nick?"

"Young. Romantic."

"I'd never have expected that of a fighter."

"It's not like you think. The boxers are the romantics. It's everybody else knows the real score. That's what makes the fighters such patsies for the money boys. I should write that in my column some day. Tell the world about it and every other ugly sore in the sporting news."

"I wonder sometimes why you don't give up sportswriting."

He searched through cabinets. "When your body works worse than a Rube Goldberg machine, you're limited. Have you come across whiskey?"

"Upper cabinet, left of the stove. Third shelf. Behind the mouse droppings. That's a cop-out. Roosevelt had polio, too."

"And he's not on the front lines, is he?"

"Who's talking about the front lines? I'm just talking about a job change. Something with normal hours. Something so you meet a nice girl."

Gal unscrewed the cap on the bottle. He wondered where that bit had come from about Roosevelt and battle, but the more he wondered the more uneasy he felt, so he shifted his attention. "I do know a nice girl," he said, pouring two fingers' worth. "Dandy lass. She shares a house with her crippled brother, has since his divorce."

Lena snapped a dish towel toward his backside. "And what happens when some Romeo proves smart enough to make me his wife?"

"There's room in the attic for him." Gal's kiss on her forehead made it clear he did not want to talk about this, and she let him go with the last word. For many years they had shared tea with milk in the morning, and he had grown accustomed to a house strewn with stray bobby pins and confusions of perfume.

Back at the table, Nick played with the letter from the attorney, sharpening the folded crease between his fingers and replacing the page in the envelope as Gal sat. Gal sipped the whiskey. Its sweetness foretold a morning hangover. He swallowed again. Once upon a time, Sophie had brushed her warm lips against the tops of his ears. Remembering that, he had the sense it was someone else she had kissed, not Galahad Simmons who walked with a cane and who was constructing a hangover in a room with a cheap card table, and chairs with patched cushions, and a wall poster of a grossly handsome pilot.

"Why weren't more people here?" Nick said. "Why weren't more people at the church?"

"The city's lousy with funerals," said Gal. "Sad as it may seem, people can't get to all of them."

"Everybody knew her. Everybody read her column."

"Sure they did. But who wants to admit that? Gossip? During wartime?"

"She wrote patriotic stuff."

"That's when nobody read her."

"At least Mr. Brainerd." Mr. Brainerd published the newspaper. "I thought he'd make it for sure. She covered all his parties, even the big ones at Saratoga or Newport. So why wasn't he around? Where were his bigwig friends she wrote about? Why wasn't even one of them at the cemetery or the Mass?"

"Those people knew her by her pen name," said Gal. "They rubbed shoulders with Sophie Diamond who wrote gossip but didn't know Sophie DiFiore who died." He thought a minute, then smiled. "Brainerd was there in spirit," he said. "Chatter in the newsroom says he paid off the bishop to get Sophie that spot in the pope's boneyard."

"Shut up, Gal." Nick pushed away from the table.

"I'm just saying—"

"Don't."

Nick closed the bathroom door hard behind him, and Gal leaned forward, elbows on the cushioned tabletop. Not for the first time that day he wished he had Sophie to talk with about Sophie's death. Hearing the bishop-Brainerd story she would have laughed—that cluck of delight she made at the most outrageous scandals—then repeated such an item in her own column, the principals properly disguised so that everyone knew who they were.

He smelled the flowers before Lena placed the vase of lilies and delphinium on the card table, and he rearranged envelopes and empty bottles to make room. She sat and fingered the stems, talking as she did. "All the way in the kitchen I heard how you upset him," she said.

"Sophie would have liked hearing about a bribe."

"He's not Sophie. Sophie's not here."

"I know that," he said.

"It wasn't good, Sophie and you together. She wasn't good for you. You were kinder before."

His fingers fumbled a moment, reaching to tug an earlobe, then to check a shirt button. Finally he eased the vase out of her reach so that she would look at him, and he smiled in a way he hoped seemed gentle and nonchalant. Ice swirled in his glass, empty now of whiskey, and he sucked a cube into his mouth, bit hard through it. "She was a magnificent woman," he said. "Always kept a straight part in her hair, you know?" It was all he could say before a shiver overtook his throat.

She touched the top of his hand, her fingers cool and dry. Her knuckles were a bit rough and her nails smooth but uneven. Sophie's had been different, with manicured nails, soft skin, hands false in their perfection. Lena said, "I'm sorry. I shouldn't have said that about her."

"No apologies for honesty."

Lena continued, though, as if to explain herself. "You never talk about her or your marriage, or why it ended. I've always—"

A crash interrupted, like the sound of a light bulb exploding. Gal hobbled after Lena toward the sound, toward the fire escape. Past her, outside, Nick raised beer bottles overhead and flung them at a concrete walk below.

The next thing Gal knew he was squirming through the window, dragging his bum leg behind him across the sill. Suddenly stuck, his foot wedged and knee impossible to lift, he called out just as Nick raised his arm to unleash another bottle. Once Nick had yanked Gal through, the men retreated to opposite corners of the platform. Neither spoke, but Nick cradled his head in his big hands, panting as he might after a fight's last bell.

Gal lit a cigarette and offered it.

"I'm in training," said Nick. "But thanks."

"Sure."

If there were clouds they drifted high and thin, imperceptible except that the sky looked whiter than usual. The air smelled of overripe pears. The sun had moved from view, and the fire escape now lay in late-afternoon shadow, which seemed to make the heat bearable. Gal pulled up his socks and noticed that the cuff of his pants had ripped when Nick pulled him through the window. "Look at that," he said.

Nick didn't look. "Sophie had enough in savings for the casket and the headstone, the mortuary bills, that sort of thing. I don't want anything else."

"Are we talking about the lawyer again?"

"I won't profit by my sister's death."

"No, you won't. It's a loss no matter how much the circus pays. A Rockefeller fortune couldn't change that."

Nick nodded in a vague way as if working out that arithmetic and finding comfort in the sum. At the same time, Gal's crippled leg began to ache. He shook it with both hands to prod the circulation. Nick said, "You ever wish you weren't 4-F?"

It wasn't a question Gal expected. "It is what it is," he said.

Nick pointed to his own face. "Every day I wish I had someone else's eye," he said. Nick's left eye, Gal had noticed before, sometimes wandered, and the pupil bled a bit into the iris. A boxing injury. Nick said, "Can you believe this will keep me out of the army but not out of the ring?" He made fists of both hands and gave them a long look. "I'd be a damn good soldier. A damn good soldier."

"Sure you would," said Gal.

"This one night a year or so ago," said Nick, "I'm walking with

Sophie downtown on Mulberry Street, after she's bought me a nice dinner, and we're dressed up, you know? These GIs come out of a bar, start giving me guff 'cause I don't wear the uniform. Said I was enjoying a pretty woman while they were out eating North African sand and getting shot at. Said I was in the pansy division. I tried to tell them, but one shoved me against a wall. Training took over, you know. I didn't want to hurt those boys."

"Did you hurt them?"

Nick pursed his lips as if trying not to cry. "Sophie, she loved it. Told me I could lead the march to Berlin if they'd let me fight."

Gal tried to imagine the scene. "How many were there?" he asked.

Nick frowned. "You don't even get what I'm saying." He took another bottle from the box and flung it at the sidewalk below. Amber glass shattered into dangerous edges, white suds spreading and disappearing into a dark muddle. Nick kept his back to Gal, facing the city, his head turning slowly as if he searched for the place where men would understand him. Gal rubbed his temples in little circles with his fingertips.

"Sometimes I think—" Gal said, then interrupted himself to start again. "It's crazy, I know. But when I heard Sophie had died, I had this sense that if I'd been able to join up, if I'd been a soldier, then she'd still be alive. It's crazy, but there it is."

Nick turned to the box of bottles but this time opened one and drank from it. His face looked different, bruised and weary and even more handsome. He said, "After the fire, they brought the bodies to the armory. That's where I had to go. They laid them out on the drill floor, each body under a blanket on a narrow little cot. The women in one corner, the children in another. Some of them burned a little, some a lot, some so perfect you couldn't figure out why they were dead. We stood in line, and we went in a dozen at a time, a nurse and a cop with each of us. The stink—God, it's still in my nose. Putrid! A woman collapsed from it right in front of me. Priests prayed at cot after cot, mumbling Latin, anointing. One body, it was so burned . . .

I saw this picture once in a magazine, this picture of a dog buried by a volcano. Lava. The dog wasn't a dog anymore. It twisted back on itself like it wanted to bite its own ass. Its legs looked all shriveled, and its mouth was open a little. You could see one fang, maybe its eye."

Nick's face had reddened, and a pulse throbbed visibly in his neck. Gal thought of dogs and of agony and of Sophie, and Nick's words, though quiet, sounded like the choking barks of a dog straining at its leash, barely words at all. "Jesus, Gal," Nick whispered. "That's what she looked like. That was her."

Gal shuddered, closed his eyes, and wiped sweat from his brow with the rolled-up cuff of his shirt. Nick's pain called to his own as if by name, urged Gal to step nearer to Sophie's brother, even to hold him and be held, but that selfsame pain repulsed him, too, bullied him into looking away. With the stump of his cane, Gal traced the fretwork on the metal grate of the fire escape. He wanted to say or do the thing Nick needed him to say or do, but what that was he didn't know, didn't even know how to learn. He said instead, because he could speak it without weeping, "You know why Sophie went to the circus? She told me before she left."

"Didn't you hear what I just told you? This is all you can say?"

"Jesus, Nick. What do you want from me? I don't know anything about this stuff. I'm no good at it."

Somewhere in the apartment building a woman laughed, long and without music. Both men looked toward the sound. She laughed again.

"I guess it's a million-dollar day, ain't it?" Nick said, and he spit at the landing, then wiped the spit with the sole of his dress shoe. "Let's go to a ball game, huh? What do you say? You and me. Who's playing tonight? You must know. Let's get seats on the first-base side. We'll forget all this. Hope to see a double play and catch a foul ball."

"That's not what I meant, Nick."

"What then?"

"Not that."

"You ever been punched?"

"What?"

"Have you ever been punched? Taken a shot. Bare fist. To the face."

"No."

Nick nodded as if that figured, as if that made all the sense in the world. He held his bottle out far from the fire escape, leaned over so he could watch it drop one, two, three floors to the sidewalk. That sound again, that gentle explosion. "I love my sister," Nick said. He stepped through the window into the apartment, hanging back long enough to say, "Stay out here a while, okay? Take your time."

Gal sat himself on a step and with shaky hands finished his cigarette. He squashed the butt on the sill, then kicked it down the steps and lit another. He knew who was playing, yes. Nobody was playing. The Twilight League had canceled its games. There was no baseball, no boxing, no bicycle racing—there might as well be no sports page. Hand over the column inches to the city desk for the circus fire or to the wire desk for the war. Gal's universe called on account of irrelevance.

He glanced inside. Lena and Nick stood near each other, Nick waving his arms about until Lena reached out and laid fingertips over his heart. A moment passed, and then the two hugged, surprising Gal with their embrace, which seemed to start as consolation but evolved into another sort of tenderness. After, Lena tucked her hair behind an ear and frowned in the most beautiful way. Behind them, the pilot on the wall still gave his thumbs-up. Everything about the scene frightened Gal.

Downstairs, some gravelly-voiced man was yelling about who made the goddamn mess dropping beer bottles and who was going to clean it up goddammit because little kids like to play out here and what if somebody had been walking along minding his own business he could have been killed some kid could have been killed and hadn't there been enough people killed didn't anybody think about that? Crows snickered as they congregated on rain gutter after rain gutter, feathers ruffling, tails twitching. A woman a floor above was stringing out laundry, a child beside her blowing soap bubbles, the wand in the girl's hand dripping, the bubbles glistening as they tumbled over the railing and drifted out and up, and out and down, following each other, at last vanishing in silent sharp breaths.

That girl would have questions one day, as would all those her age, and those children not yet born. Questions prompted by a composition for school, a photograph of a long-dead relative, a crumbling newspaper page discovered wrapped around airy glassware. Where were you during Pearl Harbor? When the troops landed in France? What do you remember from that day when the circus fell to ash?

My wife died there.

She had told him she had a ticket to the circus matinee, told him that very day when they arrived coincidentally at the newsroom's drinking fountain and couldn't avoid each other. "I want to touch a tiger," she said, and made a snarling smile and a claw out of her hand to strike at him. So he knew the moment the umpire called the game because of an emergency at the circus in Hartford. He *knew*. Why then did he do nothing except go home to sit on the loveseat in his house, bent so his forehead almost touched his knees, listening to the radio reports and waiting for Lena to come home and tell him what she'd seen in the city?

My wife died there.

He was only an ex-husband years removed, a newsroom crony, the insinuation of what had once failed. Still, he wished Nick had telephoned, asked him to go to the armory, to share that burden. Except Nick didn't call, and Gal didn't go, and now he'd never know for sure whether he would have crossed the threshold into all that death to find Sophie's corpse. "She liked how you knew so many poems," Nick had said.

Lena appeared at the window to the fire escape, her face bright and pink and alive. "We're taking a walk," she said. "Nick needs some activity." Gal waved an invitation to her, and his attempt at a smile became a pursing of lips. She looked back into the apartment, but he insisted, so she pulled herself through the window, careful with her skirt so it wouldn't snag. She slipped off her heels before settling her stockinged feet on the grate.

Gal reached for his sister's cool, strong hand, then closed his eyes, and he saw Sophie (in her own black stockings, a hat with sequins, a hair lock lacquered and curling over her jawbone) insisting that he accompany her to a party. It was a dance party, he told Lena, a twelve-piece band with the trumpet too loud, and while he and his cane leaned against the ballroom wall Sophie cavorted with a dozen young men, devastating them with her jitterbug and her foxtrot.

"We accepted a ride home from one of her dance partners," he said, eyes open now but his hand still resting with his sister's. "It was after midnight. Saturday morning. We rode in the backseat. She said good-bye to our driver by gently scraping her fingernails up and down the back of his neck. In the kitchen she dropped her purse on the floor, then leaned against the counter near the knife drawer. I wanted a scotch and asked if she wanted one, too, but she didn't answer. Instead she opened the drawer, reached in for a long knife. Not a butcher knife. Smaller than that. But bigger than a paring knife. She held it near her face. I always thought she had the loveliest face, a face Maxfield Parrish might have painted. She held the knife near her face, and she smiled as she licked the flat of the blade, once, her tongue just curling around the sharp edge, and she pulled the knife along her tongue slowly, and then she just smiled. The next day she asked for the divorce. I couldn't imagine fighting her."

Lena squeezed his hand and looked at him with such pity he wished he had kept silent, and he wanted her to go. He released her hand. "Nick's waiting," he said.

Gal smoked a cigarette to give them time to leave, then crawled back into the apartment. He cracked more ice and poured more whiskey. He drank standing at the window. Down on the street, a tobacco shop, and next door the store that sold fabric and notions. Lena and Nick sat on a stoop across from a stationer's. They sat a little apart.

Nick gazed away from Lena down the street, and Lena looked at Nick.

In the bathroom he fumbled with his zipper and pissed, then washed his hands and face in cold water and dried with a pebbly towel. Passing Nick's bedroom, he noticed boxes of odds and ends that must have been Sophie's: a Turkish bazaar of hats and handbags, knickknacks and ornamental pillows with knotted fringe, and strewn across the bed photographs and journals and letters. Gal set aside his cane and made a place for himself on the mattress edge; the bed springs creaked with warning. Almost all the pictures showed Sophie, and her impatient cursive read out from many of the pages. He shuffled photographs and letters, stopping at a portrait they'd sat for during their honeymoon on the Maine coast. They'd stopped in the studio of an untalented photographer, and Gal had the idea that they should sit with their backs to the lens. Sophie loved the photo so much she'd offered it to her editor on the society page for a wedding announcement, but the paper's policy allowed only portraits of brides. Now Gal set the picture aside and found, wrapped with a silvery ribbon, letters from when he'd convalesced at an out-of-state spa. "Exquisite Sophie," he wrote, and "whispers of our embraces . . ." "the fireflies that glow along the shore of your body . . ." Every word with which he had loved her proved familiar. Silly now, in retrospect, but still potent: a thread of diction at the end of which he found her. She lay before him in the sawdust of the tent's floor, quiet and surrounded by flames. A smudge of ash decorated her cheek, and her hair was mussed, as if after a nap. He reached for her hand, and she smiled with gratitude even as fire drew near. He felt no heat, though she did, curling herself into a ball and sometimes kicking at the flames. She kicked and kicked and clenched her teeth and growled, and he tried to lift her into his arms but couldn't with only one strong leg. Then her eyes closed, she gasped, and out of him heaved a silent entreaty that she stay. He panicked and clutched her hand, and hoped for every hopeless thing.

On the bed in Nick's apartment, he cried easily, overcome by something like peace or exhaustion. He put aside the letters he'd written. When he could search again through the keepsakes, he happened upon a letter to Sophie from a man named Hillyer. He knew who that was, though they'd never met or even breathed air in the same room so far as Gal knew. But Hillyer was a friend of Mr. Brainerd's, president of a factory that made horseshoe nails and fielded a bang-up baseball team in the city's Industrial League. Hillyer's handwriting was blocky and elegant. The letter's date placed it in the midst of Gal's marriage to Sophie. Gal blinked often to clear his eyes as he snatched at paragraphs and sentences—a knowing joke here, unadorned lust there—and he kept his lips tight and jaw locked to resist the tics that seemed intent on taking over his face. And then, not only Hillyer, but also Glazier, Delaney, Salem, Richmond. Some names he recognized, some he didn't know. She'd kept them casually, not all in one place but scattered amidst department store receipts and birthday cards and the rare recipe, as if they meant nothing, these transactions that proved the day-and-night fear he had suffered through their marriage, and since. Cuckoldry—the suspicion of which had broken him then— mocked him now on another man's bed, betrayal in words and pictures. Glamorous Sophie. Bathing beauty Sophie. Cold, hard Sophie. Alone or photographed with Gal (that cripple, that mistake), or with young, lovely, tuxedo-clad boys.

If only he had hit her. Wouldn't everything have been different? When she drew the knife away from her tongue, if only he had slapped her cheek or knocked the knife from her hand. She had wanted a fight; now he did, too. A rematch. She owed him that, and death did not erase the debt. His eyes felt huge in his head, he could see every moment of his life with Sophie, all the beauty and all the madness. He wanted her with him in this room, on this bed, to test him once again with her cruelties.

Lena's voice filled the apartment with his name. He had no time even to stand before Nick appeared, eyebrows raised in curiosity and surprise. Gal scrambled off the bed, seizing his cane and then fistfuls of Nick's shirt and pushed him against a wall.

"You've read all this," Gal spit. "You know what she did to me."

Too easily, Nick pushed him away, and Gal's head crunched against the plaster when he fell. Nick shut and locked the bedroom door. Outside, Lena shouted their names.

"I don't know what you're talking about," Nick said.

Gal picked himself up. A constellation of pain at the back of his head shined round to the front, and he staggered, catching himself on a bedpost. He scattered letters onto the floor with a sweep of his arm. "She owes me for this. I don't care if she's dead. You call that lawyer, and you get that money."

Nick turned and spoke into the space between the door and the frame. "Everything's fine, Lena," he said. "Give us a minute."

With his cane, Gal pushed himself erect, stepped close again. He forced himself to look at Nick's face, into his eyes, to accept the challenge made by a broken nose and troubled eye. Gal waited for the blow. He wanted it. "You get that money, and when you're married you buy Lena whatever house she wants."

Nick laughed. "Hey, you know. You're crazy. I hardly know your sister."

"You will. I see this future plain as day, and you're a fool if you don't. You buy her the house she wants. You hear me?"

When Nick opened the door, Lena yelled at them, and the men stepped silently into the main room. Nick circled the card table and picked a bug off the leaf of a lily. The darkness outside had made its way in, and Gal switched on two lamps. He rummaged through the closet in search of his suit coat and decided he would not repair the torn cuff of the pants. It was Sophie who'd picked the suit out and paid for it, insisted he wear it when out with her. Now he deserved a new one. One from Stackpole's, the swanky store downtown where the likes of Brainerd and Hillyer were fitted and tailored. Every man deserved such a suit.

When he was halfway into the coat, Lena stepped near to help him find the second sleeve, and she whispered a question, her breath tickling his ear. "Satisfied," Gal answered, and when she looked puzzled he cupped her chin. He said, "Are you coming along?"

"Nick asked me to help with things at Sophie's flat. He'll bring me home." She hugged him then, bringing her scents of rosewater and garlic, and he held her a long happy time.

At the door, Nick volunteered to join him in the walk down the stairs. Gal tried to shoo away the offer, but Nick insisted. For a man with a bum leg the stairs were indeed punishing, steep with unfinished boards, and when Gal slipped he caught himself on the banister and drove slivers into the heel of his hand. "Look at that," he said to Nick, and grinned, showing the bleeding drops that salted his skin. Nick asked, "You want help?" but Gal answered, "A few splinters is nothing," and started off, leading the way.

Outside, in the passing halos of headlights, Gal offered his right hand to shake. Nick's grip was strong, and Gal tried to match it. When they let go, Nick reached into the back pocket of his pants and held up the attorney's proposal. A moth flitted around his face, and he flicked it away with the envelope. "Maybe Sophie owed you something," he said, "maybe not. I don't know. However you worked your marriage was between the two of you. But she's my sister, and I love her. I told you before: I won't profit from her death." He tore the envelope and its letter in two, then tucked it back in his pants pocket. "I never read those letters, and I won't. They're yours if you want them. But let's not talk about any of this again." He looked then at Gal, and he winced in the way men do when watching the flash of another's chagrin.

Once Nick had left him, Gal crossed Grove Street into a crowd of children playing with a basketball. Under the tobacco shop's awning, a young man in uniform nearly bumped into him. At home he showered, powdered with talcum, and dressed in his pajamas. He turned on all the lamps so his house glared bright with electricity. A slipper of Lena's rested on its side near the loveseat, and its mate lay cockeyed by the living room door. She had been in a rush that morning. His hands trembled as he placed the slippers side by side outside her bedroom. Then he switched on a floor fan and pointed it at the couch where he sat with a scotch as the radio warmed up. Gal heard himself say, "I don't lie. I've been a good brother and a loyal husband." He said, "I tip well at the tavern." The urgency of those words embarrassed him, and he smiled at such silly candor. But who could hear? Not Sophie. Now sounds came from the radio, words and tones, reports from the war. He listened for a long time to news from Africa, the Pacific, Europe, until he could no longer endure the static and the faraway voices of those British newsmen.

Ellen at the End of Summer

FRANK SNAPPED OPEN THEIR BLANKET NEAR ELIZABETH PARK'S rose gardens while Ellen tended to the boy, who was not their boy, who was the age for starting school. He had blue-black hair and ruddy ears, and he stayed near Ellen while Frank opened their picnic basket, freed the sandwiches from wax paper, and took the church key to the soda bottles. Ellen asked for a plate, then arranged the boy's lunch.

It was summer 1947, a Tuesday, and Ellen and Frank, late in their thirties, had been married a decade. It was a good marriage. They had lived apart only when he was stationed in England, where he had a desk job and never saw combat. Nevertheless, she worried during the buzz bombing, and throughout his absence she longed for the physicality of him, putting his pipe near her bedside to smell his tobacco, wearing his fedora on nights out with the girls, tipping it as she imagined Katharine Hepburn might. Keeping her upper lip stiff, she tried not to think too much of the reality that he was all she had. Likewise, she tried to ignore the implication of their quiet house on Walbridge Road, but it reminded her with its rooms that were too large and too empty. They had bought it because it seemed a good place to raise children, and for many years she had imagined young voices in the hallways and upstairs bedrooms. She foresaw children as a natural extension of her love for Frank and his for her, as a way to invest the world with their happiness. She dreamed it hard, that perfect future, kept dreaming it even now when it had failed. Their first child would have been eight this summer, and the second would have been seven. The third would have been the first of the victory babies. The fourth would not yet have celebrated his? her? first birthday. With each pregnancy, Ellen's body had proven insufficient to the task until she and Frank had no choice but to accept the fact of her imperfect womb. And now, everywhere Ellen looked: babies, babies, babies.

"Careful, Teddy, those thorns will bite," she called, because the boy had gone to smell the roses, and he fingered the stems.

"He's a little old for that sort of talk, I think," said Frank. "Boys explore until they get hurt. That's what they're made for."

"I know that," she said. "But I want to return him to Ania in one piece."

When Teddy returned, he staggered toward them, his head tilted back so the plum-colored rose petals he had pressed to his shut eyes wouldn't fall off. They slipped off anyway.

Ellen laughed at him. "Teddy," she said, "what does the sun smell like?" This was a game she had taught him, one she thought was good for his imagination. She thought he might someday be a poet.

"I don't know," said Teddy. He bit into his sandwich.

"Try to imagine," she said, screwing a finger toward his tummy. "What does the sun smell like?"

"Peaches," he decided.

"And what color is your name?"

"Green," he said as he put the rose petals into his nostrils. She applauded his efforts, and he laughed. "Now," she said. "What song does a teapot sing? Sing it for Mr. Patterson."

This part Teddy always liked. Maybe a song-and-dance man, then. Her little Fred Astaire jumped up from the blanket, away from his sandwich.

> I'm a little teapot, short and stout.
> Here is my handle, here is my spout . . .

"Bravo," said Frank, and he rubbed Teddy's head. "Let's eat." Behind them was clear blue, but to the west there were clouds. The threat of rain only made the day's heat worse, stickier. Ellen wore her blouse collar open, and she noticed that only one or two women in the park had left their houses wearing nylon stockings. The women fanned themselves and pressed sweating soda bottles against their skin. Some sat on picnic blankets, others beneath the wide canvas tarpaulin the city had installed for the season, around picnic tables draped with flimsy cloths. Near an oak, a father directed children in a game of pin-the-tail-on-the-donkey. The lawns of the park seemed to sprout children. Tomboys and girls clutching dolls. A boy with two scraped knees. One with a black eye. Brown shoes and white socks. Tennis shoes. Patent leather. A girl missing front teeth. A boy keeping a downy feather aloft with furious puffs. Cowboy fringe. A hair ribbon. A girl playing a lollipop jingle on a harmonica. Freckles. Runny noses. Tears.

Ellen finished half her sandwich, and Frank sipped his soda. Teddy ate two bites and drank none of his soda. He watched some boys play with a ball, including an older boy who picked the teams, made the rules, and punished rule-breakers with a quick punch to the shoulder. Teddy watched, looking very much as if he wanted to be punched, too.

"Teddy," Ellen asked, "what game do the roses play?" Then she said, "I have paper and colored pencils, if you'd like to draw." He was good: a future Winslow Homer. But he said nothing, only fingered his sandwich, lifted then dropped the top slice of bread. Frank rested his hand on Ellen's shoulder, rubbed near the puffy sleeve, a message, she knew. They had learned to talk through touch, and she had to admit: He understood Teddy's boy-ness.

"All right," she said to Teddy. "You can play with them. But first—"

She tugged up his socks, pulled down his sleeves, made certain the white button at his collar was well fastened and that all his scars were hidden. This is what Ania would have wanted, and Ellen loved them both; it was what she wanted, too. How things change! Before the fire, Ellen had liked neither the boy nor his mother. Ania was hired help then, a dreamy Polish woman (almost a girl) who did not clean house well at all, whom Ellen had hired only at Father Dominic's urging. And later, when Ania's toddling son broke things, only Ellen's charity and patience kept Ania employed. But then came the circus of three years past, and the burning big top, and Ania and Teddy inside, and everything changed. Ellen visited them in their separate rooms on separate floors, suffering as their dead skin was peeled off, as grafts replaced it. For weeks Ellen was a link between mother and son, and she lied to both. "Teddy laughs," she had told Ania, even when he screamed all afternoon. "Your mother is almost better," she had told Teddy, though sadness gripped Ania so she slept or kept silent for hours. Ellen visited Teddy more often than she did his mother, staying with him as late as the nurses would allow. Most of her prayers were for him. He couldn't be touched for fear of infection, so she read to him. She brought in hand puppets, and she made up harmless dramas with happy endings. She colored with crayons, letting him tell her what to draw and what color to make the house and the cat and what color to draw his mother and his father (an infantryman on emergency leave; gentle with Teddy but deferential to her—even in his son's room). Teddy's favorite color then was blue. Now it was purple. Now Ellen was fond of Ania, and she loved Teddy, and she was glad to entertain him on the many days when Ania, still dreamy but a better worker, cleaned houses up and down Walbridge Road.

Off Teddy ran to join the other boys. She watched him go and worried that he would tear his shirt, or his trousers would ride up the leg in some rough boys' game, and the others would see his scars. She worried about the awful things children say. That he was having fun did not lessen her concern. Still, she was glad to feel it, because it seemed akin to Ania's concern, to a mother's concern. Ellen tried on the feeling, stepped into it, pressed her palms against its walls, pushed to see where it would go. This was a regular exercise of hers. Sometimes she spent hours in a reverie of pretend motherhood. Other times she couldn't stand it for a moment.

She knew Frank was watching her, so she turned to him. She brushed a fly from her shin.

"You could change your mind," he said. "Adoption—"

"We can't adopt him. He's taken."

"Of course not him. Another."

She took a bite of the chicken sandwich, then wiped mayonnaise from the corners of her mouth with a napkin. She swallowed before she spoke.

"I want a child I love," she said, "the way I love Teddy—or more. Aren't you scared at the thought of taking a strange child into the house? No? It terrifies me. There are so many I don't even like. Look at the bunch out there." She pointed at the boys. "Who's to say we'd get the right one? It's not like a dress off the rack. We couldn't bring it—him, her—back to the orphanage."

"You underestimate yourself," Frank said. "Given time, you could love any child."

She slipped off her sandals and turned down the brim of her straw hat to shield herself from the sun. She crossed her legs and opened Teddy's sketch pad in her lap.

"We don't come here often enough," she said. "It's so beautiful, and we live so close."

"People with children go to parks," said Frank. "And old people whose children have grown and left home."

"Don't be cruel," she said.

They sat a while without talking, looking around the park but never each of them at the same spot. Frank concentrated on the duck pond and the parking lot, Ellen on the children and the sky. Then Frank asked, "Which roses are these?" He tugged a nearby stem.

"Grandiflora," she said.

"And those?"

"Trailing Memories."

"I could cut one for you," he said, pulling his penknife from his pocket.

"Don't you dare. It's illegal."

"I've cut them before. That rose you get every morning on your birthday."

She paged through the sketch pad, past Teddy's uncertain efforts to copy white-crowned pigeons and Carolina parakeets from her Audubon book. She found a blank page and doodled with the colored pencils, drawing an oceanside landscape she had never seen, all wide beach and distant water. The afternoon disappointed her. She had expected that after lunch Frank would return to work and she would have Teddy to herself. Foolishness. There were actual boys about. Why would Teddy play with her?

Now he scrambled to escape the older boy, joy and panic on his face. When tagged, he fell, picked himself up, and with a grin and a shout started the chase anew.

"I don't know why it bothers you," she said, "having him around so much. I'd think you'd want him around, too."

"It's different for me," he said. "I don't know why, but it is."

"You don't feel age yet."

"I'm older than you."

"That doesn't matter. I feel it closer now. And I don't have the distractions of an office."

"You bought him shoes today."

"He'll need good shoes for school. The ones he has pinch."

He finished the soda Teddy hadn't touched, tilting his head way back. She could see the stubble in his skin under his jaw. She leaned forward and kissed his neck. "Thank you for my annual contraband rose," she said.

"You're welcome," he said, and he squeezed her hand. Over the last few months, their conversations had been like this: quarrels and tenderness and misunderstandings. They faced a new life, and they were trying to understand what that meant and what they wanted now.

Teddy ran back to ask for soda.

"*Please*," instructed Ellen.

"Please," said Teddy.

When he leaned over to pick up a bottle, she could see under his collar a patch of rippled, bruised flesh, like a drying flower petal. Ellen had never seen all of Teddy's scars. Though she had often washed his hands and his face, she had never bathed him. She suspected that he suffered from knowledge of his own skin, that although the physical pain of the fire had years since passed, he must wonder in confusion about his difference. She imagined that he inspected himself in mirrors when no one else was around.

Now the knees of his long pants were dirty. Mud on blue.

"He's got to be hot," Frank said. "Can't we roll up his sleeves or something?"

"Ania's afraid he'll be teased."

"They'll tease him anyway," Frank said, "because he dresses funny."

She remembered a few nights before, at a party fund-raising dinner: everyone drinking new French wines, fantasizing about a Truman visit to the state, attacking the Republican assembly for dilly-dallying when what our boys needed was more housing and bigger state colleges. "And not just a guarantee on city construction bonds!" Frank had said, nearly shouting. "Real money. Real bricks and mortar." There had been an Italian woman from Waterbury at their table, and while the men made jokes about Robert Taft and the Republicans, this woman complained to Ellen about school pageants and the extra grocery shopping and the spread of pink eye. When she asked how many children Ellen and Frank had and Ellen answered none, the woman said, "Ah, how wonderful to be free."

Now, on the blanket in the park, recalling that harpy from Waterbury, she said to Frank, "You don't want a child." She had never known this about him, but she knew it now.

"I do, if you want one."

"That hardly seems to be wanting enough."

Ellen looked at her husband, and she thought he must have seen that she was about to cry, because he reached out to cup her head with his hand. She whispered, "You want a Democrat for governor more than you want a child." She couldn't hold back now, and the back of her throat felt clogged with phlegm; her eyes burned though damp. He fiddled with her earlobe and her earring, then leaned forward and kissed her cheek. "You can't stop me from buying him shoes," she whispered. "I won't let you. If I love him, then I love him, and you have nothing to say—" She cried some more, and she smelled the piney scent of his cologne and was angered by his constancy and glad for it. He shifted on the blanket so he was closer to her, and she gritted her teeth as he put his arms around her. She rested her head on his shoulder, and sooner than she expected she relaxed into the familiar feel of him, and he let her stay there until she'd had enough.

"I'd best get back to the office," he said. He cinched his tie. He kissed her forehead at the hairline. "I'm already late," he said. "Try to get home before the rain, okay?"

She wiped her face as he disappeared among the rose bushes. He would have made a good father, damn him. She could tell because he was so gentle when she needed him, and she so often needed him, it seemed. She was struck by the idea that without a child of her own, she might always be a child herself, stubbing her toe and screaming all out of proportion, needing Frank to kiss the wound and make her feel better. But no. The proportion was right. The grief was real.

In the sketch pad she added a few tufts of grass to the beach and a seagull to the sky. The grief was real. She thought of how a week earlier, after Ania had finished cleaning Ellen's house, the two sat for coffee at the kitchen table and watched Teddy through the screen door as he studied a daddy longlegs that crawled over the steps of the back porch. Talking to the creature, he was as unaware of the two women in the kitchen as the daddy longlegs was of him. Ania smiled, as if happy to be taken for granted in this way. Then she began to say that she had never understood love until Teddy was born. Only then, because she knew how Teddy's curled fingers made her insides liquid and how she had never felt any such thing before, not even love for her own mother. That awareness saddened her, because what was true for her likely was true for Teddy. "How do I say it?" she asked. "One hundred women could never sweep clean the house that holds how much I love him. But in the room where Teddy loves me, a little dusting, a little polishing, it's done." Ania twisted the corner of a napkin, and Ellen laid a hand over hers. Ania said, "Why am I crying? I'm so happy."

Ellen closed the sketch pad just as the rain started. It felt pleasant at first, a balm from the heat, but then it fell faster and in dime-sized drops. She called for Teddy as she collected their plates and leftovers and the blanket, and by the time she reached the tarp raindrops darkened her dress over the shoulders, her bare feet slipped inside her sandals, and mown grass clung to her toes. The rain fell in curtains, faster than the ground could absorb it. She looked for Teddy in the crowd that stood shoulder to shoulder under the tarp. Other adults called out names. A dozen or more children still ran to and fro, laughing in the downpour. The older boy had stripped to his bare chest and short pants, then taken off his shorts, too, splashing around in his underpants and opening his mouth to the rain. Other boys mimicked him and stripped, all of them older than Teddy, and Ellen watched as Teddy—his hair plastered to the shape of his skull—began to do the same.

He unbuttoned his shirt and his sleeve cuffs.

He unlaced his shoes.

Now, clothed only in white underpants and socks, he looked toward the adults sheltered under the tarp. She caught his eye, and he hesitated as if worried she would call him back. But she didn't. She knew Ania would, but she kept silent. She wanted, for once, to see him as his mother saw him. So she nodded her permission, and Teddy yanked off his socks.

She could hardly see his scars. At that distance, through the heavy rain, his skin looked no worse than the tanned flesh a boy might gain from beach sun. The children kept playing, and the older boy encouraged them, waving his arms like an orchestra conductor. Around him frolicked Teddy. With the others he marched in circles. Collided in accidental hugs. Fell in the wet grass and new mud. There was whooping and squealing and the drumming of rain across the tarp. Some children escaped the shelter to join the romp, but others who tried were seized by the hand of a grown-up.

Then the downpour moved on, leaving only a drizzle in the half light of thin clouds.

The children slowed their play. The older boy seemed to realize now that he was more than half-naked in front of adults, and he scrambled for his pants. Next to him stood Teddy, his body plain. Ellen saw for the first time his collection of dimpled patches. Light purple in some places and gray in others, with the ghost lines of stitchings still visible. A collage of his brief and painful history, and so lovely.

Other children gaped, too. Teddy looked about, and in his eyes there was no panic, only surprise that the game was over, and then a slow-born awareness that he and his patchwork skin had become the center of attention.

Children arrayed around him, all wet and grassy and mud-streaked in the unceasing drizzle, questions and curiosity in their postures and faces. Some stepped from under the tarp to see the fuss. As they did, Ellen clutched the blanket, wanting to sweep Teddy into it and save him from the cruelty of children.

But Teddy seemed not to care. He grinned, and his face radiated as if inspired by some grand joke he'd heard years before. He bowed to the other children in an exaggerated way, as a harlequin might bow to royalty. And he sang to them.

> *I'm a little teapot, short and stout.*
> *Here is my handle, here is my spout.*
> *When the tea is steaming I will shout,*
> *"Come tip me over and pour it out!"*

He mimicked the teapot, one arm out like the spout, another curled to his hip like the handle. He poured. He danced. He repeated the verse and poured again. Danced his difference higgledy-piggledy with whimsy and spunk. The older boy's laughter was half-mocking, but that of the younger children sounded honest with delight.

When she gathered him wet into the blanket, and he was laughing, she could no longer hear the rain. She was filled with something louder, a passion new to her, one she'd not known through this summer or in the years before, something that could last beyond checkers and pencil sketches and new shoes that didn't pinch. Teddy laughed in her arms, and she wanted him though she already held him, longed for him and had him and wanted him still. She had never felt so completely in the world.

On the walk home they surrendered to the drizzle and let the weather slide over them. She carried his wet clothes and admired his dance down the sidewalk, his little body still wrapped in the picnic blanket. He stopped for a moment beside an elm, and he opened the blanket, looked at his nearly naked body, and giggled. She squatted beside him—"My boy!"—and opened her arms to catch him.

He did not run to her. He said, "Mrs. Patterson!" and she let her arms drop to her sides. He said, "There's a raindrop in my belly button, Mrs. Patterson!" and that world to which she had belonged fell away, carrying the boy with it, so once again she stood apart.

He squished the water out of his belly button, and she did not smile. They walked down Walbridge Road, and she did not even hold his hand when they passed the Griswolds' house where his mother scrubbed and polished the bathroom floor, her dark hair (the color of his hair, she remembered) tied up in a haphazard bun.

Son of Captain America

THE BOY WATCHED FROM HIS BEDROOM WINDOW AS THE NEIGH-
bor beat the dog. The man used a branch broken from an oak tree.
With one hand he pushed the dog by its collar toward the hard-packed
ground and with the other hit its flank with the stick. The dog yelped
and snarled, and together the sounds—the dog's, the stick's—sickened
the boy. The dog was big, and white and black, and in the dark from
the second-floor window the black part was hard to make out. But the
boy knew the dog. He had petted it sometimes. He could picture its
wet eyes, the scar across its muzzle, the fatty tumor over its ribcage
that didn't seem to cause the dog any pain even when touched. He
remembered the trash-can smell of its breath. Elbows on the sill and
palms against the window glass, the boy imagined what was happening to the dog more clearly than he could see it. Another yelp, and the
boy's father came into his bedroom.

"What the hell's the racket?"

"Mr. Nardi's hitting Tiny."

"Jesus. He's waking the whole street."

The father threw open the window. Shower water dripped off
him, and he smelled of Ivory soap. He wore a towel around his waist.
The boy's name was Franco. He was eleven years old. He called his
father Pop.

"Nardi!" Pop yelled. "Cut it the hell out or I'll come beat the hell out of you, too!"

"It's my goddamn dog!" Mr. Nardi yelled back.

"It's five in the goddamn morning!"

Mr. Nardi hit his dog again.

"Last warning!"

When Pop left the room, he ordered Franco back to bed, and Franco pretended to go. He paged through a comic book as the noise continued outside, and he read as if he were counting one-alligator, two-alligator . . .

"You—and—your—Commie—Masters—have—a—lot—to—learn—about—America!"

Through his open bedroom door, Franco saw Pop hurry down the hall to the stairs, still barefoot but dressed now in work pants and a dirty T-shirt, his face fixed in a familiar way. Franco had seen the look on comic-book superheroes who meant to save the world, and he'd often seen it on Pop, but on Pop it made Franco bite his fingernails. Mom in her bathrobe followed her husband to the top of the stairs. She saw Franco watching her and ordered, "You don't go anywhere." Then she ducked into his little sister's room, shutting the door behind her.

Back at the window, Franco watched Pop snatch the oak branch out of Mr. Nardi's hands. Mr. Nardi punched at Pop, who slipped his head out of the way—didn't even move his feet—then returned two left jabs square to Mr. Nardi's nose. Mr. Nardi fled to his house, his arms waving like he was batting at bees. The dog retreated to a corner of its pen, and there curled itself nose to rump. Franco tucked himself into bed and waited, lying still, shivering though warm, until Pop came back.

"You have to get up for school in an hour," Pop said.

"I can't sleep."

"Let's have breakfast then."

While Franco toed a slipper onto his foot, Pop gathered open comic books from the bed and stacked them neatly on Franco's dresser. His face had changed now. He looked darker around his eyes and forehead, the way Franco'd seen people get when they thought hard, and the skin around Pop's mouth twitched as if he couldn't decide whether to smile or frown. He said, "I shouldn't have hit him."

Franco checked under his bed for the other slipper. They were his favorites. They looked like Indian moccasins. "He swung at you first, Pop."

"Doesn't matter. It was easy what I did. And mean. It's easy to be mean. You gotta try for better, you know?"

On the walk home from school that day, Franco found the dog's body left in the gutter for the street department to pick up. Franco was not alone when he found the dog. He was with his pal, Dominic. They had walked home together because they walked home together every school day, because they were neighbors and buddies. That day, though, neither had spoken to the other. Dominic was Mr. Nardi's son.

When they discovered the dog, Franco's face reddened and his ears burned. The dog's mouth was agape, and its neck was twisted so that it gazed with open, tranquil, bloodshot eyes at an upside down world. The boys stood in the street. Behind them a car hummed past, then another, spent leaves twisting into the air in their wake. Dominic sighed. He bent and unbuckled the dog's collar. The tags jingled. He tucked the strip of leather into the pocket of his jacket, then disappeared inside his house.

The police asked Franco's name when he telephoned, and he gave it. They asked Franco's street address, and Franco told them 229 Preston. Again he watched from the bedroom window, this time as officers questioned Mr. Nardi before walking to Franco's house. He heard them knock, heard them ask questions, heard Pop answer. Franco closed his closet door behind him and with a flashlight read comic books.

His shield stops all bullets!
This is too easy—I suspect a trap!
Captain America! Commie Smasher!

Words, colors, crime! Mad science brought to heel. Powerful punches and final justice. The quiet moment respecting death, even that of a most villainous foe.

Pop opened the closet door. "Out," he said.

They faced each other. Pop cuffed Franco across the head so hard Franco fell to the floor. He rushed to stand again.

"We don't need the cops," Pop said. "We're decent people, and we live a decent life. They've got no business here. None. Don't you ever bring them to our door again. Don't you ever bring them to our street. You hear?"

Then Pop kissed his son and sent him to bed without supper.

Later, after the routines that ended days in the DiFiore house (Denise clicks off her bedside radio, Mom rinses the glass of her nightcap, Pop closes his book and turns out the porch light), Franco peeked out his window. From behind another pane of glass and another window screen, Dominic Nardi stared back.

Franco and his sister and Mom and Pop lived in a Hartford neighborhood that was more a village, its flat-faced houses wedged together, its needs met by a corner grocer, a post office, a city park with woods and a swimming pool, a car mechanic, a florist, and a baker. Pigeons thrived there, but not rats, and clotheslines went unused only in winter or in rain. In this neighborhood lived Polacks and Puerto Ricans and some blacks and a Jewish family or two. Mostly, there were Italians and Irish. The Irish owned houses with garages. They had settled the neighborhood first, and they ran things. Irish priests drank whiskey in the rectory offices of St. Augustine's, and they visited the homes of the parish's Italian families only when obliged by death. Irish cops made Tully's Tap their off-duty headquarters, and that was why (so the joke went) neighborhood crooks never got caught: The stink of beer sweat and cabbage farts was always first to reach the scene of the crime.

Mom was not Italian or Irish. She was an older Yankee type, a rarity in this neighborhood, of English descent with a blush of German, who had grown up among the ornate homes of Blue Hills and had quit college to marry an Italian factory worker. Pop used to joke that she chose him for his cooking. "Before me, she'd never heard of garlic," he said. Except Mom did all the cooking and always had as long as Franco could remember (his favorite: her meatloaf with bacon strips baked across the top). It also fell to Mom to steer Franco and Denise through the rites of the Catholic church, because Pop refused. He would not attend Mass. He missed all services, including Easter and Christmas and also the occasions when Franco and Denise first received the sacraments. In his life, he told his children, he'd seen things that spoiled him for God. "You give a damn, that's good enough," he often said, and he called it Pop's First Commandment. He lived that way, best as he could. If a neighbor needed help to spread asphalt for a new driveway, Pop went. When an old maid up the street didn't know the man at her door, she telephoned Pop. Long before the incident with the dog, on the day a car accident took Mrs. Nardi, Pop sat with her grieving husband and son on their porch, sharing the silence. One time Pop even stopped a policeman too zealous with his nightstick from beating up some neighborhood teenagers. He could do that sort of thing. He wasn't a big guy, but he had been a boxer when he was young—a welterweight—and in the ring he had learned things, that bleeding stops, that winning is better than losing, that the way to survive losing is to love whoever beats you. In his dealings with other people, he was never afraid. Sometimes, though, other people feared him, a reality he found upsetting because he worked hard to be affable.

The DiFiores had moved to this South End neighborhood from Hartford's Italian ghetto when Franco was seven years old and Denise was five. They left the ghetto because the city planned to raze it for a business plaza, but for the DiFiores the timing was good: They had already saved enough money to invest in their own house. They bought a two-story home, brick, with enough bedrooms that Franco and Denise didn't have to share. On the summer day the family moved, brother and sister kept each other company in the backyard of their new house. They slurped water from a garden hose and played in the shade of an oak. Denise wanted to look at her brother's comic books. Franco didn't want her to. He yanked an issue of *Robin Hood* from Denise's hands. The cover tore. Franco punched her in the stomach. Denise cried.

Pop jerked Franco into the garage. He ordered Franco to make fists with both hands, then he wrapped each fist in duct tape, the tape shrieking as Pop peeled the roll. He wrapped the fists so tightly Franco's fingers tingled.

Then Pop made Franco sit next to Denise on a bench in the backyard. Because Franco could not use his hands, Denise had to turn the pages of the comic books. Franco had to read to her. His hands ached. He beat his hands against the rusty frame of the bench for relief. He begged Denise for a glass of water, and she laughed at him.

After an hour, Pop called Franco back to the garage. Pop took a knee, then cut the tape with a pocket knife. Franco complained the tape jerked his skin, but Pop looked at him as if he knew it didn't hurt much, and Franco shut his mouth. When the last bit came off, Franco tried but could not unball his fists. He could not unfold his fingers. All pink and mottled and useless, his hands seemed to belong to someone else.

Pop said, "Only cowards punch girls."

Franco, who had always thought of himself as one person, became two on the day he and Dominic found the dog in the gutter. The collar tags jingled and Dominic vanished behind the Nardi door and Franco divided. One of him followed Dominic inside the Nardis' yellow house. That Franco walked heartbeat-for-heartbeat beside his friend as Mr. Nardi, still dressed in his insurance sales tie and shirt, shadowed his son up the stairs to the boy's room. The knot of the tie was loose and crooked, its red tails flopping over Mr. Nardi's belly, and his collar was dark where he'd sweated into it. At the bedroom door he shouted, "You got a question? You got a question?" then slammed the door between him and his son. For hours he kept shouting and breaking things, and he left the TV on with the volume loud. When all that stopped the silence was scarier.

The other Franco, the one left on the street, ran home so fast that pencils shook out of his book bag, and he left them on the sidewalk where they fell. That other Franco called the police and later got whacked with an open hand that made his head ring.

When Franco woke the next morning he wandered about his bedroom sifting through papers in his desk, rummaging through his closet, peering under his bed, then staying by the window and watching the Nardi house a long time. He studied himself in the mirror as he brushed his teeth, but he saw nothing unusual, no parts missing. His skin hadn't changed color, wasn't more ghostly. He dressed (favorite plaid shirt, navy pants, sneakers with old chewing gum flat on the soles), and he snuck a comic book among his school books to keep himself from getting bored during math. At breakfast, nobody gave him a once-over as he expected they would. His mother didn't ask whether anything was wrong. Denise ate Cheerios with bananas and sugar and read the back of the cereal box and ignored him. Pop sipped his coffee and read the newspaper. When he finished, he knocked with his knuckles on the tabletop. He said, "Look, you two. New rule. No going inside Mr. Nardi's house. No matter what. You hear?"

He didn't have to say why. Denise nodded and turned back to her cereal, but Franco watched his father. Pop, as if anticipating Franco's question, said, "You and Dominic can stay pals. But he invites you inside his house, say you'd rather play at the park or something. Be polite, but don't set foot inside that door."

That morning, Franco met Dominic and walked with him to school. They tried not to look in each other's eyes. In class Franco teased a girl because she was rich, and he doodled on his penmanship lesson, and at recess he played Smear the Queer, and everything was as it always had been. The walk home with Dominic happened in silence, and Franco was glad for it because he didn't know what was right to say. This lasted more than a week. Then the quiet became boring. So one day after school, Franco stopped Dominic before he could start up the walk to the Nardi front door. He said, "We can hunt down the man who killed your dog. We can search the yard for clues. We can bring the killer to justice."

Dominic led the investigation, dividing the front and backyards into quadrants and deciding who would search each. When Franco found something, a smashed paper cup, a bag from a hardware store, he brought it to Dominic who decided whether it was truly a clue. Afternoon light became dusk. Dominic had chosen four things he said could unravel the case: a footprint, a cigarette butt, a license plate recovered from the duff beneath a lilac hedge, and a tangle of fishing line. The boys placed the clues, except for the footprint, in the overturned lid of a metal trash can and contemplated them.

Dominic said, "It was my Dad."

"No," said Franco. "He didn't have a motive."

"I'll see you tomorrow," said Dominic, and he hurried inside.

Eventually, Franco and Dominic agreed that whoever killed the dog had escaped. It was too bad, but he would turn up again. Such was the way of villains. Meanwhile, there arose other threats to the world. Mrs. Vovonovitch. Mr. and Mrs. Hayes. Mr. O'Connell. All villains. Either evil scientists or communists or mobsters or Nazis. The boys spied on each, sometimes sneaking around their houses, other times pedaling bicycles past, popping wheelies or riding no-hands, pretending to be nothing more than boys. They might even wave hello. But later, at night or in the early morning or when the day grew muggy and grown-ups shut themselves indoors, the boys worked to right the scales of justice. They'd snip every stalk in a bed of poisonous daisies, or they'd destroy the secret lab in a neighbor's house by running garden hoses through a cellar window and turning on the water. "Go home Commie" they'd paint on a fence. They fought evil throughout the neighborhood, ranging blocks away from home. Each successful adventure emboldened them to another.

One summer evening, lying in dead grass behind a scruffy rose hedge, the boys spied on fat Mr. Schwartz, whose German name gave away his Nazi sympathies. "A war criminal," Dominic whispered as Mr. Schwartz cut his lawn. "Escaped from the Fatherland as the Americans marched into Berlin. With that mower he sends secret messages to his masters in Argentina." Franco crushed a beetle with blue-and-green wings that had been crawling on his shoulder, then flicked away the remains. "If the Nazis take control of Hartford," he whispered, "New York will be next to fall, and then the whole country." The boys watched Mr. Schwartz steer his mower into a shed at the back of his property, comb his few strands of hair with his fingers as he admired his work, then enter his lair. When they heard the rush of shower water through an open window, it was time to act. First they captured the mower from the unlocked shed. Then they wheeled it through yards and alongside fences to Goodwin Park where Dominic had hidden a baseball bat and a claw hammer under bushes in a wooded area. "We have to destroy the mower," he said. "There's no other way." He used the bat. Franco wielded the hammer. They took turns swinging and smashing, the crunches and ringing of the dying mower muffled by brush and trees around them. Twilight dimmed as they worked, and they sweated in the slick summer air, and the boys couldn't recognize the mower after a while, its push handle mangled, its wheels severed from its body. With the claw end of the hammer, Franco smashed, smashed, smashed into the gas tank, and gasoline spurted over his hand and arm. He stank, even after he washed using the garden hose in Dominic's backyard. He scrubbed again in the industrial sink in his family's cellar, powdering his arms with Ajax cleanser. Then, with an invented sneeze and sniffle, he escaped to bed without kissing Mom and Pop good night. He turned out the light without paging through a comic book. Under his sheet he twisted right, then left. He looked out his open window into the night. It had begun to rain, and water smelled hot off the asphalt streets, and crickets fell silent. Through the smell of bleach, Franco noticed now and then the sweet scent of fuel, and it reminded him of the evening's heroics, the fear and the thrill, the single-mindedness of their purpose, the abandon in their arms.

The signal was Dominic's idea. When he needed to alert Franco to a new adventure he'd tape a five-pointed star, cut from black construction paper, to the inside of his bedroom window and leave a light on. When Franco saw the silhouette he knew to ring the Nardis' doorbell twice and run and wait for Dominic at home base: a garbage dumpster outside the motorcycle repair shop on Franklin Avenue. One August night the black star appeared, and later, leaning against the dumpster, Dominic pulled a brown bottle from inside his jacket and uncapped it. "Super-soldier serum," he said, and he drank a long gulp, then handed over the bottle. Franco smelled the beer. The glass was cold in his hand. He sniffed the lip. "Go ahead," said Dominic. "We'll be stronger and faster and better fighters." Franco nodded, and together they drained the bottle, belched and giggled. Dominic smashed the empty against the dumpster, shards of brown mixing with the grit of the pavement. He howled like a wolf, and Franco howled, and then the two wrestled and laughed and wrestled some more, their sneakers scuffing in the grit and the broken glass, until Dominic pinned Franco against the dumpster.

"Isn't your mother German?" Dominic asked.

Franco stopped smiling. "Only a little." He waited for Dominic to say what they both knew he meant to say. But Dominic didn't speak, and Franco said, "Just because she's a little bit German doesn't mean she's a Nazi."

"I just wondered."

"How did you even know?" Franco pushed free of Dominic, then stepped away from the dumpster. He breathed hard to recover his wind.

"I just heard. That's all."

"It's not a big deal."

"It means you're German, too."

"Am not."

"Mein Herr!" Dominic shouted, and he shoved Franco with both hands so that Franco had to catch himself on the rough wood of a telephone pole. Dominic stepped forward as if to do it again, and he howled, and Franco ran. "German!" Dominic yelled. "German! German!"

The Black Star Adventures ended when Franco began high school at South Catholic and Dominic at Bulkeley, the public school. Now, mornings, Franco walked south and Dominic east. The black star made no more backlit appearances in Dominic's window. Franco joined CYO basketball, and he pitched for the South Catholic junior varsity. He made new best friends, boys whose parents sometimes visited the DiFiore house, who played cribbage with Mom and Pop and called them Lena and Nick. He visited these boys in their homes and ate lunch with them or sometimes supper. Sometimes on the way to a game or to practice, Franco saw Dominic—arguing with Mr. Nardi in the yard, or in the driveway fiddling with a carburetor—and Franco waved, or didn't. He remembered the Black Star Adventures as mischief-making: fondly, with embarrassment and pride. He confessed them in church, asked forgiveness, and prayed his penance. The priest absolved Franco and answered his one question: No, the boy did not have to tell his father.

This was the time in his life when Franco didn't want to tell Pop anything, not even something so routine as Mom needing him at the supper table. Franco did not want to be seen with Pop. He turned down the old man's offers of rides home from practice, and he volunteered for other chores to avoid a drive with Pop to the hardware store. It was not that Franco hated his father or disliked him. It was not that Pop's breath smelled of coffee, cigarettes, and blood, or that his eyebrows grew long and unruly, though both were true. It was not those things, or maybe it was, or a combination with others. Franco couldn't figure it out, didn't care to. He knew only that he had an animal's instinct to escape whenever Pop was near.

In late spring, Franco found himself waking early. He'd visit the bathroom, then crunch through a bowl of cereal while sitting on the porch. Morning air smelled clean, without the clutter of exhaust or coffee or onion simmering somewhere in butter. The quiet allowed him to hear the ticking of the refrigerator, the sighs of the house, the slap of newspapers against porch steps. Mornings brought his imagination to another world, a planet without sisters and schools, a place he alone possessed. But he was not the earliest riser, and Pop would eventually return from his daybreak run, sweaty, in a V-neck T-shirt and gray gym shorts, tube socks drooping. Pop stretched his muscles, then sat with Franco and unlaced his sneakers. They talked if there was reason—about school, about boxing, about potholes on Preston Street or about some game Franco's team had lost or won the afternoon before. Sometimes Pop told family stories, about Franco's sportswriter uncle who won big at a horse track in Arkansas and never came home, about their aunt Sophie who had died in a circus fire of all things and was the reason Pop stayed away from church, about a distant cousin who bought a new car every time a woman broke his heart. If they had nothing to talk about, Dad tuned a transistor radio to an AM station, and they listened to Hartford begin its day with broadcast jokes and music, amid the songs of finches and chickadees and a distant thrum of tires on Franklin Avenue.

These mornings, Pop, somehow, became bearable—even interesting. Franco noticed that when Pop breathed through his nose, broken flat by a right cross in '47, the nose made a little whistling noise. He saw how Pop's hair curled in the spots where his daily dab of petroleum jelly had been sweated or washed or wiped away. He marked that Pop said, "Well—" and clapped hands before lifting himself from a chair. Franco looked at his own hands and wondered how long before his thumbnails would grow so thick and his palms so callused.

This daily interest in his father, the mystery of Pop, persisted until someone—Denise, Mom, a neighbor out to walk a dog—interrupted, and Franco bolted from the porch to shower and pick out clothes for school.

Then it was summer and school ended, and Pop asked Franco whether he might like to join in the run.

"Get up a little earlier," Pop said. "I start with calisthenics. Might get you in good shape come football season."

They began the next morning in the cellar with one hundred jumping jacks. Then Pop unfolded gym mats, and they each counted off fifty sit-ups and forty push-ups, which Franco could only finish by taking them in groups of ten. On the front sidewalk, father and son stretched. Then they launched themselves into the city.

To Goodwin Park where they followed the lane around its edge for a mile, then up the hill they had tobogganed in long ago winters.

Then Cedar Hill cemetery where they rested that first day near the monument of Samuel Colt the gunmaker, and later by that of J. P. Morgan, whose name sounded rich. When they crossed a pond with lily pads, Pop pointed out deer and a heron and wild turkeys.

Along Fairfield Avenue with its houses of many windows and porch columns and sprawling yards. Down the hill at a bushy blue hydrangea on White Street, then home. When Franco asked why they only ran through the South End's pretty places, Pop said, "You want to run through a dump?"

After a few days, Franco could finish the loop without stopping. Then Pop ran faster, so Franco did, too. Then faster again. Franco met every new push, ran stride for stride with his father, panted when he panted, breathed easy when he breathed easy, rolled his neck mid-run as Pop rolled his neck. Franco kept secret how he sensed himself grow taller each morning, faster and stronger, running alongside Pop and becoming someone who could parade among the monuments of great men and be applauded.

One Sunday, Pop ran straight at the White Street hydrangea.

Franco turned as usual, then doubled back. Did Pop forget? The next block then. But Pop turned the wrong way, heading farther from home. Franco sprinted to catch up but drew no closer than to see the dawning sun shine off Pop's sweaty skin, to see the colors of his shorts and T-shirt. A left turn. A right. Nearer West Hartford. Now Pop added distance between them. Franco grunted and picked up his pace. His knees shivered each time a foot slapped concrete. Pop ran through neighborhoods Franco didn't recognize, along streets he'd never visited. Franco shook his face to keep sweat from his eyes. A leashed dog snarled and charged as he passed its yard; all Franco heard was his own panting. Pop added more distance. Now he turned a corner and Franco couldn't see him anymore. Now he could. Across railroad tracks. God damn! Shit! Franco's lungs swelled bigger than his chest. Franco's lungs turned to stone. What was Pop doing? What was he thinking? Franco hated Pop but couldn't let him go. He did not think to stop. He did not think to turn home. He chased, he stumbled. He fell forward, step after step . . .

Pop stood outside a diner, waiting. He grinned. Franco gasped, "What the fuck?"

"Don't use that language with me," said Pop, but his tone sounded easy, happy.

Franco doubled over, leaned with elbows on his thighs. His stomach was in his throat. Pop took him by the shoulders, straightened him up. Franco couldn't focus his eyes, couldn't stand, couldn't lie down. Pop's breath felt hot on his skin. Pop looked into Franco's eyes, and Franco tried to blink him away but couldn't. Pop said, "What a warrior." He cupped the back of Franco's head with his open palm, pulled his son near. "It embarrasses you," he said, "that I love you. Okay. But listen. You chased after me. You followed when I went the wrong way, and out here, away from your friends and sister and mother, I can tell you this. You love me. And I love you that much and more, Franco Di-Fiore. That much and more."

Franco opened his eyes. Lights flashed and Pop's face looked blurry, then clear. Franco blinked hard, then looked again. Yes, Pop was crying. He had never seen Pop cry. Pop made no effort to hide his tears. He said, "French toast and bacon?"

After breakfast, Pop put a coin in a pay phone. "You better come get us," he told Mom, "or Franco will miss Mass."

Franco did not miss Mass. And he ran with Pop through the summer. Then in August the football team started its annual two-a-day practices, and Franco pleaded exhaustion and skipped the morning run. After practices fell off to one a day, Franco still slept late. Pop ran alone.

★ ★ ★

Franco turned sixteen. That fall, on a Friday night, he showered and shaved and slapped his cheeks with aftershave. He dressed in a fake silk shirt and black dungarees. He knotted the laces of his shiny leather shoes. He gargled mouthwash, and when he spit in the sink it was a spit of disgust. He was unhappy. No one in the DiFiore family was happy.

He'd had plans: a community dance sponsored by the Knights of Columbus. A night for joking with pals and flirting with Catholic girls from the public schools. But then the telephone rang, and it was the Gentinos inviting Mom and Pop for cribbage, and Mom accepted, and then Franco had to explain that he had plans, too, and so he couldn't hang out with Denise the way he usually did when his parents went out for an evening. Denise lifted her arms as if beseeching God and complained. "I'm a high-school freshman," she said. "Why can't I be trusted on my own?" But Mom and Pop didn't trust her, and they told Franco to stay home, which Franco complained about until he found himself begging to bring his kid sister to a dance. Imagine that.

Mom and Pop talked it out. They didn't like their decision; they worried that Denise was too young for her first dance. But all right.

When the time came to leave, Franco went to fetch Denise from her room. He knocked, but she didn't answer. He called upstairs and down and from the back porch. No reply. He circled the house, looked up and down the street. Now he looked over to the Nardis' yellow house, the rain-sodden couch, the dented gutters, the weeds that choked its gardens. Dominic's window. A light there and from the kitchen. Damn. Maybe it was true, what the girl from Denise's confirmation class had whispered in his ear.

At the Nardi front door Franco didn't knock, because he wanted to surprise them. Knock, and they'd run away. He popped his knuckles, then turned the knob.

How many years had it been? He stepped through the unlocked door and into darkness. The house was not what he remembered, and it was not like his house, which Mom kept well lit, which smelled of garlic and teenage-girl perfume and fabric softener. The odors of this house spoke of ashtrays and sweaty shoes. The only light came from the back of the house, a narrow and harsh sliver that stabbed into the living room where he stood. It cut across a coffee table, across Mass cards and prayer pamphlets that were creased open, reaching finally to illuminate a birdcage in the corner. The yellow-and-red bird inside called *chirr-ip chirr-ip* and pecked at seed on the tinny cage floor. Franco pulled the door behind him but didn't close it, reached into his pants pocket, reassured himself that he had the jackknife he always carried. Somewhere a radio played at a cozy volume, a familiar voice asking, "Anybody want to give blood? Anybody? It is in short supply. All types, but especially B-negative and O-negative are needed." The bird scratched at its feed. *Chirr-ip! Chirr-ip!* Franco thought of the dance, of letting public-school girls touch his curly hair, of lighting their cigarettes. He stepped toward the brightness, careful with each footfall so he wouldn't stumble in the dark. He walked on his toes to keep his leather heels from tapping.

He didn't recognize her at first, because he had never seen his sister sitting on a kitchen counter, blouse dangling though still tucked into her skirt, bra shiny in fluorescent light, the cup of the bra, the lift of her breast. She looked beautiful and perfect, his sister: her back arched, dark hair loose and bouncy, skin pale, her neck long and muscled and still bearing the thin gold chain and crucifix she'd received for her confirmation. She whispered. She whimpered. Breezes from deep inside her crossed the lips she offered *him*.

Who was blue-jeaned and shirtless, hunched over her like a skinny, hairless dog with its face in a bowl, growling, and pressing his fingertips into her skin . . .

The lovers broke their grip and looked at Franco as one, as if the roar in his brain had been loud enough to distract them. Denise shrieked and dropped off the counter out of view. Dominic did not act so startled. Had he even looked surprised? He leaned against a wall. He took a cookie off a plate left on the counter. As he chewed, he slid his already unfastened belt free of its loops and wrapped the leather around his right fist so the metal buckle lay across his knuckles.

"Franco," he said. "Not a word, buddy. Not to me. Not to Denise. Not to your old man. Not to nobody. Not now. Not ever."

Franco said, "We're going to a dance. She's supposed to come with me to a dance."

"Didn't I say 'not a word'?"

"You need to come with me," said Franco to Denise, who had edged back into view, still bare-shouldered. She shook her head.

Franco turned to Dominic. "We're late already," he said, distressed by the pleading in his voice. "The dance started. She's got a ten o'clock curfew."

Dominic smashed his belted fist into the plate of cookies, crumbs and shards everywhere. "Didn't I say 'not a word'?"

"I'm not going anywhere," said Denise.

"You know Pop's rule."

"I know all of Pop's rules."

Dominic laughed. "*Don't go in the Nardi house*," he said, jeering, and he lifted his open hand as if it were the grasping claw of a Halloween monster. "*They're scary, those Nardis. OoooooOOOOoooo!* Now here comes Franco the hero to rescue his sister. We're fine, buddy. I'll get her back by ten. Meet us for a grinder at Franklin Avenue at half past nine. My treat."

"Denise, you don't want this. C'mon. This isn't right."

"Go away!"

"You're outnumbered, cowboy," said Dominic. "Best run git the sheriff."

Franco flipped him a middle finger, then headed for the door. In the living room he stumbled in the darkness, grabbing a doorknob and yanking it. A puff of cool air hit him, but there was no street, only stairs to a basement.

"Wrong door, hero," said Dominic, and he pointed across the room.

Dominic and Denise arrived late to the grinder shop, too near curfew to order a sandwich. Franco played with the wrapping paper of his Italian-sausage-hold-the-fried-onions, watching through the shop window as Denise did not kiss Dominic good-bye but instead swiveled her hips in a way that suggested more than kissing. Franco stepped outside. The streetlights hummed.

"Sorry we're late," Dominic said. "Here's a couple of bucks for the grinder."

"I'm not afraid of you," said Franco.

"Yes you are. But for now Daddy's got your back."

At home, Franco followed Denise onto the porch, the two of them passing Pop's book, face down, the spine cracked. In the kitchen, Pop sat at the table paying bills. Denise poured orange juice over ice and lied about where they'd been, how they'd driven around in Joey Rome's Impala listening to the car radio, how they stopped for grinders, then walked to Bulkeley for the dance but were glad to keep curfew because Franco noticed a gang of Irish boys there, and you know those Irish boys: They're trouble.

Franco looked at her as if *she* were trouble, and Pop must have noticed because after Denise left the room he said, "You'd miss her if she was gone."

"I don't think so," Franco said, but he remembered Pop talking about his own sister, the one who had died in the fire, and he knew Pop had reasons for what he said and did that Franco might never understand. Pop said, "It's important you look out for Denise, keep her out of harm."

Franco said nothing, but later, after staying up late enough to watch test patterns on TV, he paused by Pop's door and listened to him snore, not an easy rhythm but an off-pace, sudden and violent snatching at air. The sound kept Franco awake through the night.

Dominic lay on a couch in the Nardi basement, working an imaginary throttle and gearshift, crowing about this guy Evel Knievel— "Yeah, that's his name"—a motorcycle daredevil who jumped cars. It was November 1967. Senior year. Franco listened from a nearby easy chair that had been patched but still leaked stuffing, and he tossed a baseball from hand to hand. They'd become friends again. Denise had a new boyfriend, and Dominic and Franco forged a truce over cold tequila and their shared plans for life after high school, which were no plans. They had in common small paychecks: Franco from his work as a night janitor for a machine-screw company; Dominic from a part-time job at a motorcycle repair shop. They greased their knuckles together on Dominic's motorcycle, a cheap, wimpy, broken-down British bike that they could get to run every fourth or fifth day. They called the bike Mrs. Vovonovitch, or Mrs. V. For his assistance, Franco received rights to Mrs. V three nights a month. Now and then he convinced a girl to join him for a ride.

In the Nardi cellar that night, Dominic drank tequila out of a jelly jar and chased it with a can of beer. They could hear above them voices from a television, Mr. Nardi watching *My Three Sons*.

"No shit," Dominic told Franco. "This Evel guy cleared sixteen cars at a show in California. He's gonna jump fountains at a hotel in Vegas on New Year's Day. I can see me in that life. Black leathers. A helmet that shines in the sun. Badass boots."

"Can you wear that stuff in Vietnam?"

The night before they'd eaten Chinese takeout, and when they read the fortunes from their cookies, each of them added ". . . in Vietnam" to the end. *Generosity and perfection are your everlasting goals in Vietnam. An unexpected windfall will be yours in Vietnam.*

"Maybe if we get tattoos they won't take us," Franco said. He tried bouncing the baseball off the concrete floor of the Nardi basement.

"Are you shitting me? I want to go." Dominic reached into the drawer of a nearby table. He pulled out a handgun, checked the magazine. "Shoot me some gooks."

Franco had never seen a gun in the hand of someone he knew. He stopped tossing the baseball and pushed back into his seat. "How'd you get that?"

"I know people," Dominic said. "I bought it last summer after the craziness in the North End. Better to be prepared."

"They weren't mad at you," Franco said. "They rioted because of the cops."

"Everybody's mad at everybody. Way of the world. So I'm ready. I'm always at the ready. That's how you grow up when your old man is weak." He sneered at the ceiling. "You have to be strong yourself. You wouldn't know that. Your old man is strong. So you grew up weak."

"Fuck you."

Dominic giggled. "I'll bet I can take your old man down with a squeeze or two of this Big Bertha."

Franco smiled back at Dominic, a smile he hoped said, "You're crazy, and I'm not playing," but he pressed his feet hard against the floor as if ready to leap.

Dominic returned the pistol to its drawer. "I've got keys to the shop," he said. "Let's take a joyride. *Find bad guys.*" He sneered that same sneer. "For old time's sake. Whaddaya say?"

★ ★ ★

Some rich guy had brought in two motorcycles and given the shop a blank check to juice them. "Honda Scramblers," said Dominic as he and Franco circled the bikes. One motorcycle shone blue, the other red. A little wing marked the left and right of the fuel tank. Chrome fenders. Twin exhaust pipes. The bikes leaned forward like greyhounds.

"Three-oh-fives," said Dominic. "We lengthened the swing arms, lowered everything so there's about four inches of clearance. Put on new struts. Souped up the engines. They're hot rods on two wheels." He handed Franco a leather jacket out of a closet. Franco fingered the collar.

"C'mon," Dominic said. He zipped his. "No one will notice. We always take bikes on test drives, make sure everything runs smooth."

"What about helmets?" asked Franco.

"More fun without them."

The bike lurched forward under Franco, yanking away from him when he touched the throttle. "Sensitive son of a bitch!" he shouted. Dominic grinned, then led them away from the shop toward downtown's high-rise lights.

They dawdled as Franco grew accustomed to the machine. Old Mrs. V whispered when she ran, but the Scrambler screamed. Franco was still toiling herky-jerky with the Scrambler's throttle when Dominic started to launch himself from red lights turned green, cranking fast enough to lift the front tire, then leveling out at the posted miles-per-hour. He wove in and out of traffic, and Franco strained to stay with him, pushing his speed as far as he thought he could, then pushing it more, faster than the law allowed. Then they ran easy through the city, the night air cold, the engines hot, and Franco imagined the envy of people stuck in clumsy cars or forced to walk—so slow— while the lights of storefronts and crosswalks flashed in his peripheral vision, fleeting constellations, and Franco riding the rocket.

Downtown now and Dominic slowed near a curb, then eased the bike up over it. He pointed to Constitution Plaza, the concrete business park raised over the ruins of the ghetto the DiFiores had first called home. "Been a while since you played here, huh?" yelled Dominic. They filled the air with silver exhaust as they rode in circles around concrete water fountains, slalomed between saplings, spun donuts and jerked out of them into straight roaring thrusts, hot rubber tires leaving tracks on the clean concrete and a smell so strong they could taste it. Now and then they paused near each other and howled, then hurtled off again.

The police lights painted the drab concrete plaza in red and blue, so brief as the boys raced past, and pretty. The officers arrived on foot and in cruisers, and they aimed heavy flashlights, and shouted when Dominic and Franco shot away.

Through red lights and stop signs they shot through the city, Dominic leading the way and Franco following, not wanting to run and not wanting to stop and not knowing what the hell else to do. He followed Dominic without knowing where they were headed, but he figured it out soon enough and thought, "He's crazy." Franco looked behind him as they turned onto Preston Street, and the police remained too close so Franco gunned past their houses, past Dominic, glancing only a moment to his left, where he saw the porch of his house lit, and Pop with book still in hand, a dark figure stepping away from the brightness to better see the trouble.

Through alleys and parking lots. Through schoolyards and people's lawns. Franco looked over his shoulder now and then to see whether Dominic stayed with him, looking for that single headlight, too often glimpsing police flashers farther behind. Tires tore up grass and screeched on pavement, and twice on corners the bike started to slide away, but he heaved and leaned and pulled it back. Along the river, amidst factories and warehouses, he cut the lights on the bike and ran in the dark, feeling his way by memory and instinct, not looking over his shoulder anymore but trusting that Dominic would follow. In an alley he skidded the bike behind a parked freight truck and stumbled away, down stairs to a cellar door where he crouched and tried to hold his breath. Dominic hurried in beside him.

"Jesus," whispered Dominic. "Let's do that again."

Franco's legs trembled. His arms trembled. He swallowed to keep from vomiting. They waited and heard police sirens pass the alley and fade. Franco counted to thirty, then counted to thirty again, and, when he stepped out of the doorwell, unzipped the leather jacket and beat it against a cinderblock wall.

"Hey, we need to return that," said Dominic. But he stopped talking when Franco shoved him against the wall, his hand around Dominic's throat. "No!" Franco said. "It doesn't go back. We dump it. We dump the bikes. We dump everything."

With his jackknife, he cut the handlebar grips. He reared back and chucked each one in a different direction, then went to work on Dominic's bike. "God damn, that was stupid," he said. He laughed. "God damn!"

They took the bikes to the river and pushed them off a promontory into a deep eddy, the bikes splashing into water and garbage, then sinking, ripples receding into the dark. They put stones in the pockets of the jackets, stuffed them in the sleeves, and tossed them in, too. Then, at the motorcycle repair shop, they threw bricks through the display windows and ran pell-mell away, hoping that what they'd left behind looked like a burglary. Blocks later, they stopped to catch their breath. "I need to eat," said Franco.

At the grinder shop, Franco ordered meatball. Dominic had sausage. Dominic wore red sauce at the corners of his mouth. He grinned across the table. He said, "You felt it, didn't you? You understand it now. When we were kids and did stuff, it was like you were only going halfway. But when you took off on that bike tonight, man—" and Dominic howled right there in the grinder shop so other people turned and shook their heads.

Franco didn't howl. He didn't need to. This wasn't like Schwartz's lawnmower. This was real. Franco knew what he was doing when he kicked that motorcycle to life. He sped away from the cops knowing what that meant. He followed Dominic onto Preston because he wanted to, even knowing Pop would be on the porch. Dominic was right; Franco understood now how easy it was, how much fun. He wanted to keep racing police and stealing and bullying Dominic into walls, which is why he wouldn't do any of it anymore.

"You want a soda?" said Dominic. He was crouched over the table with its red-and-white checkered cloth, half standing, ready to fetch if that's what Franco wanted.

Franco shook his head no, but said nothing. He said nothing for a few moments, and when next he noticed Dominic, Dominic's expression had changed as if something about Franco surprised him. His jaw had gone slack, his eyes wide and static, his cheeks blushed. Franco recognized the look, or thought he did. He remembered one like it from the day they had discovered the dog in the gutter. Franco, who had been afraid, thought then that he saw something fearful and forlorn in Dominic's face. Probably he did see that. But now he remembered, or imagined, with greater clarity his friend's childhood face, and Franco recalled love, maybe, and loyalty, and Dominic's abrupt knowledge of what he had just inherited. That face must have contained more than fear and misery, because Dominic did not run away. He opened the door of that yellow house where his mother no longer lived and his dog no longer lived, and he stepped inside where his father waited.

Franco knew what he'd done when he roared past Pop standing on the porch. He knew what awaited him back home. He'd walk through the door ready. And if he lost, if he took a beating, he was ready to love Pop even more.

"You sure you don't want a soda?" asked Dominic.

"What the hell. Why not," said Franco, and Dominic looked grateful, smiling as he counted out his change and signaled to the teenager behind the counter, an underclassman Franco recognized from school, who wore a paper hat and a boy's happy, ignorant frown.

Mrs. Liszak

TEN MINUTES INTO THE MOVIE AND THE ONLY SEAT LEFT WAS
in the front row. Suzanne Randall thought that was where the old
woman should sit, the one who had come in late clutching a pillow
and carrying something in what was either a pillowcase or a large
pouch, and who stood watching the movie from the aisle. Now and
then the woman peered around the theater as if pleading with the
darkness to offer her a seat. Her helplessness distracted Suzanne. Apparently it also distracted her date, an Eagle Scout with pink knuckles and a '75 Firebird who was the nuns' favorite at South Catholic
High School. He had asked her to the movie, Suzanne believed, only
because it was saintly to spend time with the girl who had no parents
and no car. Suzanne's sister had said, "Any guy on a Friday night," and
badgered her to go. But now her date excused himself and left his seat
to show the woman to the one that was empty. Suzanne watched the
Eagle Scout point, and then he and the woman spoke in whispers, and
then the woman started toward the vacant seat beside Suzanne. The
Eagle Scout shrugged an apology before heading to the open chair
down front.

The woman's old-lady perfume preceded her. She bumped Suzanne as she arranged herself: an elbow here, a knee there. Just when it
seemed the woman would settle down, she opened her bag. She took

from it packages wrapped in wax paper. Whatever was inside stank of garlic. Suzanne hated the woman.

"She said she couldn't see from the front," the Eagle Scout explained after they found each other in the lobby. "She asked to trade seats. She's older than my mother. What was I going to do?"

They saw her again as they stepped from the theater into the Hartford night. Cars inching through after-movie traffic steered around her, and drivers honked as she strode the center line of Washington Avenue, caught in the now-and-then headlights. At the bright moments Suzanne could see her clearly, and the woman's straight back, her head carried high, made Suzanne dislike her even more. She wore heels and a neat skirt and a puffy blouse. Her hair—gray and black, thick, unruly—added to a sense of majesty Suzanne hadn't noticed in the theater. What power, she wondered, could make such a woman appear helpless in the aisle? Drivers yelled at the old woman to get out of the fucking road.

"Of course," said the Eagle Scout, with sudden recognition. "That's Mrs. Liszak."

Her? That was Mrs. Liszak? Even though Suzanne had been in the neighborhood only a year, she had heard of the woman with the scar. She had been burned in a famous fire years ago, people said. Now she did odd things like play hopscotch by herself or waltz without music on street corners.

In the center of the street, Mrs. Liszak smiled as she tried to thumb a ride from teenagers steering toward a kegger or to the reservoir to neck. The Eagle Scout frowned, and Suzanne knew he wrestled again with the dilemma of date versus duty, but she said nothing when he called out to Mrs. Liszak, who accepted his invitation. The Firebird had only two doors, and Suzanne meant to keep her spot in front, so after some hesitation Mrs. Liszak squeezed into the back, pushing aside cassette tapes and dirty chamois and bringing with her the odor of strong garlic. She thanked them. She spoke with an accent—Russian or something, Suzanne thought—and seemed not to think it odd that they would know her name and offer her a ride.

"Where to, Mrs. Liszak?" said the Eagle Scout.

"Take me someplace beautiful or someplace strange," she said. "No place dangerous. Strange or beautiful only."

"What about home?" said the Eagle Scout.

"Strange or beautiful only," she said again.

They drove with electric guitars loud on the tape deck and the windows open. Suzanne gazed out her window, trying to ignore the Eagle Scout and their surprise chaperone. The Eagle Scout fiddled with his mirrors, his attention here, then there, as if he were watching for the dripping, toothy monster from the movie. It had been a scary movie, but not frightening to Suzanne, who had been too aware of gasping teenagers and Mrs. Liszak's garlic to lose herself. This was how it was with her and theaters. Nothing on the screen ever convinced her to leave the crowd.

Now the Eagle Scout drove them through boring downtown, then past the winos at South Green, then onto the Silas Deane Highway. There they passed the gas station where Suzanne sat twenty-eight hours a week in a glass booth, taking money and writing down license plate numbers. She thought of the reservoir and necking.

"I see these streets all the time," said Mrs. Liszak.

"I won't take this car into the North End or Frog Hollow," said the Eagle Scout. "They'll steal the hubcaps while we're moving."

"How about Massachusetts?" said Mrs. Liszak, and the Eagle Scout barked.

Suzanne turned, said as if giving an order: "Buy us some beer."

"Bad idea," the Eagle Scout mumbled to the steering wheel.

"I only brought money for the movie," said Mrs. Liszak.

Suzanne put her hand on the Eagle Scout's corduroy-covered thigh. He owed her for this terrible date. "You have cash," she said. He looked cuter now that he was nervous.

After a stop at a package store, they parked across from Trinity College. The Eagle Scout led, a blanket he'd pulled from his trunk rolled and tucked under his arm like a football. Suzanne wanted to hurry, but the Eagle Scout made her wait so that Mrs. Liszak, slower in her heels and her age, could keep up. They passed from dark place to dark place to avoid the college cops, but once happened into a lighted archway, and Suzanne noticed then the dull lavender-colored scar that covered half of Mrs. Liszak's forehead and spread around her right eye down her cheek. Because stealth and speed were important, Suzanne stole only a few glances; she thought the scar seemed exotic and revelatory.

The college's lawn sloped away from its Gothic dormitories into a comfortable darkness where they spread the blanket and peeled open beer cans and sat watching the city lights. They kept silent for a long time until the beer and the night sky turned them toward talk. Mrs. Liszak judged the lawn and the surrounding campus to be beautiful but not so strange. She revealed that she was not Russian, no: Polish. Suzanne announced that she wanted one day to have a dog. Then she told the others that she forgave them, that there were worse things to do on a Friday night than drink beer with a neighborhood flamingo and a cute guy. Mrs. Liszak said she liked being called a flamingo. The Eagle Scout sipped his fourth beer and swiveled his head, keeping watch like the nervous man in the movie whose nervousness meant he would die next. Suzanne used the Eagle Scout's lap as a pillow, and his cologne made her crave licorice. She wished his hands toward her, even just to rest on her, but he kept hold of his beer can, sipping. Now and then the three of them paused to consider the echo of car speakers, the backfires that might have been gunshots, or the sounds of insects and small animals rustling near them in the grass.

"I have seen the largest rat," Mrs. Liszak said.

The Eagle Scout looked around. "Where?" he said.

"Behind the typewriter factory on New Park Avenue," said Mrs. Liszak. "In a culvert. She came out of the storm drain while I watched. She didn't creep. She wasn't careful. Her tail is thick as a tree branch. Her fur shines. Her black eyes are as big as yours. There is no rat larger. Not in Puerto Rico or Siam or East Germany."

Suzanne laughed. "How do you know it's a her?" she said.

"Because only a woman can be so magnificent."

The Eagle Scout giggled. Mrs. Liszak reached across the blanket and tapped his head with her knuckles, as if rapping a door. "You're a smart boy," she said.

Then the Eagle Scout and Suzanne argued whether Sister Katherine, who taught history, was a bitch. Mrs. Liszak translated into Polish phrases from the movie ("I wonder what happened to the rest of the crew?" and "Lucky, lucky, lucky, lucky, lucky"). They discussed the examples of the saints. Suzanne asked about Mrs. Liszak's husband. "The only strange and beautiful thing he loves is me," she said. "I always come home. He never worries." She did not speak about her scar, and Suzanne did not ask. Nor did Suzanne give away anything of consequence about her own life. Though Mrs. Liszak was seductive, she also seemed untrustworthy, perhaps even greedy. Suzanne kept her own pain like a treasure.

Later, after the Eagle Scout bragged that this was the first time he'd ever been drunk, Mrs. Liszak took his car keys. She drove, even though the Firebird was a stick shift.

Outside Suzanne's house, Mrs. Liszak left the car and met Suzanne on the moonlit sidewalk, promising that she'd see the Eagle Scout to his door. "Thank you for sharing this night," she said to Suzanne, then stepped close, tickling Suzanne's cheeks with strands of her unruly hair. She kissed Suzanne's lips.

Mrs. Liszak hummed something flat and out of tune as she walked back to the car, and Suzanne thought the melody funny and beautiful. She drew a circle on the sidewalk with her toe. The Eagle Scout offered a thumbs-up out the passenger window as they drove away; the taillights of the Firebird described their trail.

In bed, Suzanne licked her lips to recall the kiss. The surprise of it had stayed with her as she undressed, as her head rested into the pillow and she pulled over herself a stiff polyester sheet. The kiss played childhood games inside her and invited her to play along. Her own lips were softer than Mrs. Liszak's, but clumsy, not so proficient. Mrs. Liszak's kiss had been quick and casual, like a handshake—but happier. Her breath had been spiced with garlic and beer.

★ ★ ★

The next morning it rained. Suzanne lay in bed until the night's beer and the rainwater running along the gutters forced her to the bathroom. As she peed, she could hear the TV through the door, but not her sister's voice, or that of her sister's husband. She washed her hands and face and noticed a new pimple near her hairline, which she wiped cool with a cotton ball dabbed with rubbing alcohol.

Suzanne lived with Karen and Howard and their little girl, Chryssie, on the third floor of a three-family house east of Goodwin Park. Theirs was the only family living there: the second-floor tenant had recently been evicted, and the old woman on the first floor was hard of hearing and had her meals delivered by St. Cyril's. The building was like all the three-families in the neighborhood—rectangular, flat-faced, home to pigeons—except that from their back porch hung a weather-faded banner trumpeting the Oakland Raiders. Suzanne lived with Karen because their mother had bled to death in the hours after Suzanne was born, and through the ensuing years their father prolonged his grief through gin and became helpless. The day Karen turned eighteen she eloped with Howard, and nearly two years later, Suzanne, then fifteen, moved in with them. She hadn't wanted to, but Karen needed help with Chryssie, and their father encouraged it. Then he sold the house and moved away. Suzanne and Karen only learned this when a cashier's check arrived with a note. The note did not say where Mr. Randall had gone. "Love each other," he wrote. "Think kindly of me." Karen told Suzanne to toss the note in the trash. With the money Karen paid debts that had come with her baby girl, bought a new used Z-car, and invested in savings bonds to pay for Chryssie's college. Karen put Suzanne's share in the bank and used it to pay the tuition at the Catholic high school. The rest, she said, Suzanne would receive when she turned eighteen.

Suzanne did not miss her mother. How could she when she had never known her? Her mother was to her a curiosity, the explanation for her red hair and milky skin, but little else. She imagined left-handed people wondered about being right-handed in the same way she wondered about growing up with a mother. She knew people pitied her, and she had the sense that she'd lost something—a security, or a snugness, a confidence that other people took for granted—because she'd had no mother. She felt her mother was not even hers. Mrs. Randall, in her death, belonged solely to Karen, who sanctified her mother's memory, and who still wept for her with no warning, and those tears made for hard silences between the sisters.

When Suzanne came barefoot from the bathroom that morning she found Karen at the table cutting grocery coupons. Howard sat in his rocking recliner with an ashtray balanced on the overstuffed arm. He studied maps in a road atlas, looking up now and then at the Saturday morning cartoon on the television. He'd lost his production line job a few months back and hadn't been able to find another. But he had a friend who'd moved to California and who had once made Howard a standing offer of work. The preceding week Howard had called him and accepted. He planned to leave Monday.

Chryssie, who was two and a few months, lay in the middle of the living room carpet on her belly, scribbling with crayons on construction paper. Suzanne said hello to everyone, but only Karen replied. Suzanne said to Chryssie, "What about my kiss?" and Chryssie said, "No."

In the kitchen, Suzanne poured her morning Mr. Pibb. "You came in late," said Karen, walking near. Gently, she turned Suzanne by the shoulders, peered at her pimple, and put cool fingertips against the skin. Suzanne thought again of Mrs. Liszak and realized she remembered no time when she and Karen had kissed, not even a cheek peck. Now she jerked forward and kissed her sister's lips.

"What's wrong with you?" Karen said. She laughed and looked as if a dog had licked her face. "What's that all about?"

"It's too quiet this morning," Suzanne said. "Are you and Howard fighting?"

"No. There's just little to say now." Karen examined the pimple. "This one looks ready to pop."

"You're thinking of going to California," Suzanne said.

"Howard's going, not me or Chryssie."

"I don't believe you."

"You made me choose," Karen said. "You better appreciate the choice I've made."

"Howard's the one who chose."

It was cruel to say so, and not even true, really, and Suzanne wanted to take it back. They had often all three talked about California. Jobs paid more, Howard said. He wanted to raise Chryssie in a place where the sun shined. Karen wanted California, too. But Suzanne refused to leave Hartford. When she thought of leaving, her insides felt strangled. She had the sense California would shrink her to invisibility, make her impossible to find among all those people and lanes of traffic and that relentless good weather. She could not abide the idea of never being found.

Now Karen turned her back, and Suzanne felt selfish, and she felt worse when Karen reached in the fridge for an orange, which she handed to Suzanne. "Enjoy breakfast," Karen said.

On the back porch, rain pop-popped on the roof. Suzanne sat on a rusted lounge chair without a cushion, and the springs squeaked. Howard had left another ashtray there, and she moved it to the top of some cardboard boxes filled with empty cans and bottles, saved for the nickel deposit. She checked out the neighborhood. Her new habit involved spying on neighbors from the porch. Most seemed harmless or dull. But there was also the bald man who lived alone and sat on his porch at night without any lights on. And the young woman who wept with her curtains wide and windows thrown open. And the olive-skinned couple who sometimes had visits from the police. Suzanne had not had a porch like this in the house with her father, and they hadn't lived near so many neighbors. She never knew this pleasure until she moved to Hartford, but now it seemed necessary that she spy on customers from inside her glass booth, that she watch fellow students and teachers from the back rows of her classrooms, that she see the neighborhood from her high perch. Suzanne spied on everyone and drew their faces in her sketchbook, which she kept with a box of colored pencils and a sharpener in a satchel that had been her father's in the army. She drew half a dozen faces a page, or one on a page, and sometimes she drew people with photograph-like reality and other times if it seemed more real she turned them into Nile Queens or Mongol warriors or zoo animals—baring their lips to show fangs, or making them howl. She drew Chryssie and Karen and Howard, too, sketching them from different perspectives: Howard's lollipop face from the right and above; Karen's with its too apparent skull straight on, but from below. Suzanne filled pages of spiral-bound pads with people: crowds and crowds as ugly and beautiful as she could make them, and when she couldn't make them beautiful or ugly she added word bubbles so her badly sketched faces could admonish her: "Draw, you lame weasel!" She never shared her drawings, and at school her "No, you can't see them" ended all overtures of friendship. So what. Friendship meant less to her than the faces; she feared that students who saw them would talk about them, and their words would rob the faces of their magic. She could not say why, but she knew she depended on them. When not drawing in the book, she paged through it, recalling the attention she'd given each face, the decisions she'd made as she captured it. This felt to her something like love. Now she sharpened a lavender-colored pencil and brushed away the shavings, then found an empty page.

Suzanne sketched a tiny Mrs. Liszak. Then another. Small versions, trying to get the face right—its majesty, its helplessness—trying to remember the scar. From one angle, she drew it like a kidney. From another like a splash of ink from a leaky fountain pen. Once like half a butterfly.

★ ★ ★

She was scheduled to work Monday when Howard meant to leave. She had been glad to get out of the apartment because he wouldn't speak to her, and Karen was red-eyed and busy telling him what he needed to pack ("Do you have your umbrella?" she asked. "What about your mustache trimmer?"). Business at the gas station was slow, so Suzanne sketched more Mrs. Liszaks and worried that Howard might after all take Karen and Chryssie with him. She thought about Howard so much that afternoon that she wasn't surprised to see him park his Chevy Impala at Pump No. 8, regular. She put her pencil on the register and watched. He wiped his forehead and retied his shoe as he waited for the tank to fill, then topped it off for an even six dollars. Suzanne waved as he approached the booth, but he ignored her. She said, "Hi, Howard." He only slipped the money through the cashier's well. He never blinked. As he backed away, he looked at her, then saluted with an "Adios, pardner" kind of wave that made her mouth go dry.

Once, months before, as she climbed the stairs to the apartment, glad to be home from work or school (she'd forgotten which), Howard had stumbled past her, his face red and twisted, Karen's sobs trailing after him. Howard paused only long enough to say, "You'll wreck our marriage." Then his boot heels pounded the stairboards and the downstairs door slammed shut. When he was gone, Suzanne could still see the hate in his face, more powerful than anything she'd known, greater than what they taught at church or school, passionate enough to engulf the stairwell with fire. Now, from the glass booth, as she watched him drive away from his wife and daughter, those words returned (*You'll wreck our marriage*), and they echoed over the hours even as she slipped her time card into the clock and heard the mechanisms punch.

In the apartment, she found Karen yelling at Chryssie to stop screaming, to stop making so much noise, that if she didn't stop making so much noise Mommy would be very angry.

Suzanne waited by the door. She waited for Karen to say something.

"Please take Chryssie out of here," Karen said. "I can't stand it right now."

"I'm sorry," said Suzanne. She lifted Chryssie, whose shoes were

untied. Chryssie kicked-kicked-kicked, and one shoe fell off her foot
to the floor. "I wanted him to change his mind," Suzanne said.

"If she's here and she's screaming I can't talk to him," said Karen.
"He's supposed to call when he reaches Pittsburgh."

★　★　★

Suzanne searched the phone book for *Lishack*. Then for *Lyshack*.
Then for *Lichack*. Then for *Lisiak*. Nothing in the phone book resembled the name, so she called the Eagle Scout to ask how to spell it or
if he knew where the woman lived, but he said he couldn't talk to her
anymore, not since his old man found him asleep on their stoop that
Saturday morning, smelly and sick and still wasted.

She looked for Mrs. Liszak at Mass. In the glass booth at work,
she waited for Mrs. Liszak's face to appear. On the way to the park
with Chryssie, they sometimes walked blocks out of their way to read
mailboxes for names that might be Liszak. She knew what the school
counselor would say: "You think about this woman all the time because you want her to be your mother." But that wasn't true. Suzanne
wanted to watch Mrs. Liszak. She wanted to study her. There was
something in the way Mrs. Liszak had moved through the night; she
seemed only to gain things, she lost nothing. Eventually, in August,
on the way to work, Suzanne stopped at the local Polish deli and said
to the woman behind the counter: "Do you know a Mrs. Liszak?" The
woman laughed. Charlie's wife, she said. They live on Barker Street.

That night was damp and dark. Suzanne carried her satchel, and
she walked slowly enough to count the address numbers on houses. A
nearby streetlight and the moon shone on the Liszaks' house, which
itself was lit by a porch light. Suzanne could see the house clearly. It
reminded her less of a city house than of those in the suburb where
she and her father and Karen had lived. It was two stories, with deco-
rative shutters and shiny windows and a trimmed lawn. An apron of
marigolds encircled an oak tree. A bird feeder shaped like a steepled

church stood nearby, along with two painted roosters. The property was bordered by rose bushes and a waist-high chain-link fence. The gate was latched. No car sat in the driveway, and the sidewalk mailbox sported stenciled letters spelling out the family name. She thought it must be the house of a retired man, and in fact Suzanne saw an older man sitting alone on the porch. She noticed him only when he waved—the friendly wave of a retired man—and she nodded by way of returning the courtesy, then hurried away, embarrassed to have been caught spying and disappointed that she couldn't have lingered.

From California, Howard sent packages with money. He sent Polaroid photographs. He wasn't a letter writer, and long-distance cost too much. Instead he recorded himself on a cassette tape, and he and Karen mailed it back and forth. Karen would take the tape player and lie on her bed to listen—sometimes cuddling with Chryssie, sometimes alone. She listened to the same recording twice, three times. The voice that haunted the apartment was not Howard's, but a robot's, full of clicks and scratches, careful and distant, unlike what they remembered and too much like it. This voice tried to assure Karen, and she listened over and over as if waiting for the assurance to take hold. "I'm making a bundle out here, you wouldn't believe it," he said. "In California, sweet girl, the sun shines, and you can buy Coors, and the Raiders are on TV all the frickin' time."

The apartment had never been comfortable; it grew worse. Karen stopped at the laundromat less often, and she never folded, just took clean, wrinkled clothes from the basket as she or Chryssie needed them and told Suzanne to do whatever. She threw fliers away without cutting coupons. If Suzanne didn't wash the dishes, they stacked in the sink and on the counter and stank and lured cockroaches from the drainpipes. When light bulbs burned out, they stayed that way. The four chairs around the dining room table became three when a chair leg broke and Karen left the pieces on the sidewalk with the trash. Every weekend, Karen took Chryssie for drives in the Z-car. At first they left and returned before lunch. But then they stayed away past lunch and then past dinner. And then it was not just the weekends, but also after work.

Each time Suzanne came home and found the Z-car missing, she locked the front door behind her, then searched room to room for what might have vanished while she was gone. She made a checklist of things Karen might take should she leave: the framed Sacred Heart that had been their mother's; high-heel shoes stacked in apple crates; a Polaroid on the kitchen bulletin board of Suzanne and Karen at Misquamicut beach the day they traded bikini tops; Chryssie's polyester quilt of pastel tulips and daffodils. Only when Suzanne was satisfied that everything was in its place could she relax and paint her fingernails or watch game shows or sit on the porch, drawing faces and spying on the bald man who sat in the dark or the young woman who wept. She ate bags of noodles that cooked in five minutes, and she drank Mr. Pibb.

When Karen and Chryssie came home, Suzanne tried to sound nonchalant, said, "Hey strangers, how'd the day go?" Karen shrugged her answer, and Chryssie wanted to play with dolls. Then the two would go away again.

A golden dusk in late September and once more the Z-car was gone. Suzanne, off the bus from work, turned away, unwilling to face the empty apartment, to count proofs of Karen's presence, then wait to hear Karen's key in the lock. She walked instead, envious of people she passed: a pair of joggers, girls jumping rope, a family she spied through lit windows who fought with gestures and loud words even as they shared a spaghetti dinner. Halfway to Barker Street she wondered whether she should have left a note for Karen but decided Karen deserved none.

She rang the Liszaks' doorbell, and Mrs. Liszak's husband answered. He was flat-faced with horn-rimmed glasses and brown eyes that suggested a practiced capacity for patience. He stood stooped but strong, his fingernails thick and his hands scaly, coarse hair graying on his knuckles. He wore suspenders with his pants and an old dress shirt with the cuffs tucked inward once, as if he wanted them out of the way but not rolled in the manner of a cowboy or tough guy. Suzanne smelled something sweet coming off him, perhaps pipe smoke. She asked for Mrs. Liszak.

"Ah, the girl who thinks Sister Katherine is a bitch," said Mrs. Liszak. It sounded funny, hearing an old woman say *bitch*, and Suzanne wanted to hear Mrs. Liszak say it again. Karen, playing mother, had always said Suzanne was too pretty to let such ugly words cross her lips.

The porch light shone, and for the first time Suzanne could see clearly Mrs. Liszak's face. Suzanne hadn't gotten it all wrong in the sketches, but she had concentrated too much on the scar, drawing a gargoyle rather than a woman. She could see now that the scar wasn't so pronounced. Instead she noticed that Mrs. Liszak's face had been pretty once, perhaps even beautiful, and she decided to draw it that way next time. Sketching an old person, she had learned, meant drawing two people at once: the aged one and the one hidden by age. The scar, she guessed, had in Mrs. Liszak's youth enhanced her beauty. But now the scar mattered less when matched against her yellowed teeth or the lines notched over her upper lip.

"What brings you to my door?" asked Mrs. Liszak as her husband stepped back inside. "Would you like to come in?"

Suzanne chose between truths and said, "I want to see the Rat Queen."

"Ah, no," said Mrs. Liszak. "A waste of time." She stepped onto the porch and leaned low to read Suzanne's name tag on her work uniform. "Suzanne," she said. "I'd forgotten your name. Sit, Suzanne," and Mrs. Liszak eased herself into a rocking chair webbed with neat, taut nylon.

"Really, I'd like to see the rats," said Suzanne.

Mrs. Liszak again waved Suzanne toward a chair. "Do your parents know you're here, asking an elegant woman to take you to see rats?"

"Yes," said Suzanne.

"Liar," said Mrs. Liszak. "No parent would agree to such a thing."

"They're out of town," said Suzanne.

Mrs. Liszak pulled her shawl tight against the cooling evening. She wore high heels now, as she had at the movie, and a skirt with a lacy hem that frayed.

"Who takes care of you when your parents are gone?"

"I have a sister. But I'm sixteen. I can handle things."

"The largest rat had testicles," said Mrs. Liszak. "It wasn't a woman after all. I was very disappointed. Where are your parents visiting?"

"California."

"We have a son in North Carolina," said Mrs. Liszak. "What shall we do instead of the rats?"

Suzanne reached into her satchel and brought out her sketchpad. "Let me draw you," she said.

"What a tremendous idea," said Mrs. Liszak.

Mrs. Liszak turned off the porch light, then faced the windows that cast brightness from inside. "This is better lighting, don't you think?" she said. She hummed again the out-of-key melody from the night of the movie. Suzanne thought of carousel horses limping toward the end of a ride. She began to shape the face, but right away saw that she'd made a mistake. She turned to a new page.

"In the movie we saw," asked Mrs. Liszak, "did it scare you when the baby monster exploded from the man's chest?" She sat with her back straight, her bosom lifted and out a bit. From inside, the television made sounds of gunplay and doors smashed open and screams.

"No," said Suzanne. "It was the coolest part."

"Did any part scare you?"

"It was just a movie," Suzanne said.

Now and then she noticed Mrs. Liszak trying to hold her pose and at the same time watch Suzanne work. Suzanne decided not to turn again to a new page, but to push through her second effort, which was failing, too. In pencil, Mrs. Liszak's earrings looked to be hanging from the ends of green onions.

Mrs. Liszak's husband opened the porch door, bringing a tray of sodas and a bowl of potato chips. "Chef Charlie at your service," he said. "Everyone wants to capture the woman with the scar. Drawings. Paintings. Photos." He laughed. "I've got a scar, too," he said, and he lifted his shirt so high it covered his face. Blind, he traced with one finger a pink welt across his abdomen. "Appendix," he said. "I've also got a ripper on my calf from a rock that shot out of my lawnmower. Wanna draw that?"

"There's room for only one star on this stage," said Mrs. Liszak, "and one face on that page. You are dismissed, Kazimierz."

"Madam," he said and blew her a kiss before exiting.

So Suzanne was not the first. She wondered if others had this much difficulty. How had they re-created Mrs. Liszak? She imagined sketching her with a willowy face, like those of the ballerinas painted by the man obsessed with dancers. She imagined her as a Virgin Mary from the Renaissance, a radiance from heaven sanctifying her scar. Suzanne played with the colors, trying with purples and oranges to capture the energy around Mrs. Liszak's eyes.

"How did you get the scar?" Suzanne asked.

Mrs. Liszak stopped humming her out-of-tune melody. "I do not like to tell the story," she said. "I don't even tell my son, and he was there."

"So make one up. Like the Rat Queen."

When Mrs. Liszak spoke, her voice was conversational, matter-of-fact, as if she had told this tale a thousand thousand times. But Suzanne heard something like pride, too, at owning a story so much in demand. "No," she said. "This one is true."

The circus staked its tent outdoors on Barbour Street that hot July day nearly four decades past. Nobody knew then what made the fire. Nobody knew since. But the tent burned. Fire flew up the walls, glided over the canvas, consumed it. Fiery pieces of the tent collapsed into the crowd, like Hell, the white fires of Hell, the heart of a furnace, windy, roaring. Animal cries came from the mouths of lions and elephants and people. Children. Children in tears and panic, children who were knee-high and waist-high, crawling over the rag-doll bodies of the dead. The dead in piles near the animal chute. The dead in piles near the tent walls. Mrs. Liszak could not remember whether she had wanted to die, but she lived. Her son, Teddy, who was then only three years old (and Suzanne thought of Chryssie coloring on the apartment floor), also had not died. It was an old story, Mrs. Liszak said, and though she sometimes thought the memories were gone, they could still—when she least expected them—bring her to her knees: the brassy shouts of the circus-band trombones; the squeak of rubber-soled shoes as the nurse came to peel Mrs. Liszak's charred flesh; Teddy's strangled breathing in his hospital bed.

Suzanne penciled a brown shadow near the nose, paying less attention to that than to the thought that someone had rescued Mrs. Liszak and her boy. Someone must have dragged them away. Suzanne imagined purposeful hands (and saw the thick, scaly hands of Mrs. Liszak's husband and saw her father's), and she envied Mrs. Liszak.

"Who rescued you?" she asked.

Mrs. Liszak shrugged her shoulders. "I never knew."

"Did someone hear you yelling?"

"I can't remember."

"But you survived."

"We were fortunate. Others were not."

It was not what Suzanne wanted to hear, and she felt a small start of anger. She studied her sketch. She needed a red pencil, but when she looked she couldn't find one in her satchel.

"But you have this nice house," she said. "You have your husband."

"What has that to do with the fire?"

What had that to do? Everything. It had everything to do with the fire. On the night of the kiss, Suzanne had watched as Mrs. Liszak gained things: a seat in a crowded theater, a ride, companionship, an evening that was strange and beautiful. How? How had she been among those who survived the fire? What made her different? What quality gained her this husband, this home? Suzanne had thought (or sensed or hoped) that what had scarred Mrs. Liszak's face had also taught her this trick. Suffering brought help. Pain had power to attract those rescuing hands. It must. You just had to know how to use it. But now all the old woman could say was, "We were fortunate. Others were not," as if all suffering—Suzanne's, too—were an accident, a coin flip, a dice roll. She could lose forever.

Suzanne found the red pencil but stopped drawing. Mrs. Liszak noticed, then stood as if the sitting were ended. She stretched: an invitation, it seemed, for the world to inhabit her body. That night's kiss had convinced Suzanne that Mrs. Liszak would share her secret of loss and gain. But now, everything about her seemed to be an act. Look at her, Suzanne thought. She pretends the world owes her, but what did it take from her in that burning tent? A mother? A father? No, nothing. Nothing. In the accident that was the world, Suzanne had lost more, lost faster.

She snapped her red pencil. "Why did your son leave you?" she said. "Did he hate you?"

Mrs. Liszak looked at Suzanne the way Karen had in the days before Howard left.

"He went to college in North Carolina," she said. "Then he got a job there."

"He could have gotten a job here," said Suzanne. "He must not have wanted to come back to you."

"Aren't you cruel," said Mrs. Liszak.

"No!" cried Suzanne, as she stuffed her sketch pad and pencils into her satchel. "No, I'm not. I'm not!"

Later, home from Barker Street, she saw that there was still no

Z-car downstairs. Inside, too, she found no one. Gone from their places were their mother's framed Sacred Heart and Chryssie's quilt of tulips and daffodils. But on the tabletop: five twenty-dollar bills, a bankbook with a balance of more than four thousand dollars, and a note in Karen's perfect handwriting.

"Forgive me" was all it said.

That night Suzanne lay awake. She turned out her light, hoping to sleep, but heard clawing she'd never before noticed from inside the walls. She tried to ignore it, but the clawing persisted, and she imagined rats there, climbing the pipes and the two-by-fours, gnawing through the plaster. She turned the light on, and the sound stopped. She brought a pillow from Karen's bed into her own and curled herself around it. She heard the old house gurgle and click. She imagined Karen and Chryssie bloody inside the Z-car that had been wrapped around a telephone pole. She imagined Howard in a black rage at the apartment door. Suzanne's eyes watered from sleepiness. She listened for clawing inside the walls, and when she heard it, fumbled the light on again. She stepped to the kitchen, switching on every light along the way. She drank a beer Howard had left. She imagined rats nesting in her box spring. It was just past two in the morning. Then it was 2:05. 2:06. 2:06 again. She played the radio, but the sound exaggerated the emptiness of the rooms. She called the station to talk with the DJ.

"Hey, you sound kind of sweet," he said.

"I am," she said.

"I've got to change a record, but don't go away," he said, and while he was gone she hung up.

She tried to finish homework. She found her first-confession rosary and tried to pray. She prayed for daylight, squeezing the beads so hard they left red marks in her skin. She brought Mr. Pibb and stale popcorn and a carrot into her bedroom and shut the door and then watched the shut door, suddenly afraid of what it hid from her.

In the morning, she stayed home from school. When the telephone rang, she startled, then stared as it trembled on the wall.

★　★　★

Suzanne had been alone for three weeks. Karen had written her a dozen or so letters, and in some she pleaded with Suzanne to pick up the phone. The letters told her how wonderful California could be for a pretty girl, one who was smart, too. Bus tickets weren't much—Suzanne could pay out of the savings account.

Suzanne always felt tired. Dark splotches appeared around her eyes. Her hair went unwashed. She ate only bags of noodles and chocolate bars. She skipped school. At work, she pressed her face against the cold glass and played a radio loud to stay awake.

"You need coffee or something?" said a man outside the booth. She leaned away from the cold glass, opened her eyes. He was bald and high-cheeked and familiar. Something about his posture, maybe, or the slope of his shoulders. He slid his gasoline dollars into the well. "I could get you coffee."

She counted out the five and two ones, put his change back in the well. He reached at the same time. His fingertips grazed hers.

"You live on Cromwell?" he said. She recognized him now. It hadn't occurred to her that while she was spying on the bald man, he had noticed her, too.

"I live on Chester. We're neighbors. So, can I fetch you that coffee?" He smiled. He peeked at her breasts—no, maybe her name tag. How old was he? Twenty-four? Thirty-eight? She couldn't tell because he'd shaved his head, and he looked athletic. A jogger, probably. He wore sneakers. She noticed that he drove a Japanese pickup, the bed filled with tools and sloppy buckets. A house painter. She shook her head: no, no coffee.

When she punched out that evening, she saw his truck parked across the street at the grocery store, too distant to tell whether he was in it. She watched his truck from the bus stop, watched it until the bus had carried her away. She thought of walking home a different route, told herself to grow up, then turned down Chester toward home. He spoke to her from the darkness of his front porch as she passed.

"What happened to that Raiders banner?" he called out. "Aren't you a fan anymore?"

She hesitated before she said, "It was my brother-in-law's."

"So he's not a fan anymore?"

She gave him a half smile, waved and walked on, hurrying a little. As she turned the corner, she glanced over her shoulder. The bald man followed, a house or two back. She walked faster.

"Kenny Stabler's a great quarterback," he said, loud enough that she could hear.

She started to jog. Her house was only a few away. She looked back, but he wasn't running. Just walking, hands in the pockets of his shiny sweatpants, as if he were out for an evening stroll. At the top of the stairs, she tried to find the keys in her satchel, throwing out everything else—her sketchbook and all her pencils tumbling over the steps. Her hands shook, and she missed the keyhole once, twice. She heard the door open downstairs and heard footfalls on the steps. Then she had the apartment door open, and she slammed it behind her, twisted the deadbolt, ran the chain. "Oh God," she said. "Oh God." Suddenly, she worried that someone was already in the apartment. She didn't know which room would protect her and which room was a trap. He knocked on the door. "Suzanne? Did I do something wrong?" he said. His voice was soothing, quiet. "Did I scare you?" He knocked again. She remembered the back porch—had she locked it before work?— and ran to check. He was still speaking through the door when she came back, but he spoke so softly she couldn't hear him. She drew closer, leaned near the door. He said, "I'm sorry if I scared you. I was just making small talk. I only walked after you to apologize. I wouldn't do anything to you. My name's Weinbaum. You know where I live. Why would I do anything to you? I was just trying to be nice. You're right to lock the door. That's what your parents would want you to do. You're a good kid. A smart kid. I'm sorry if I scared you."

"I'm fucking calling the cops!" she yelled.

She felt her heartbeat in her throat, against her eardrums, in her fingertips. She realized she had been crying, the taste of salt on her lips. She crouched low at the door and listened. His voice frightened her, but it was so calm, so comforting, that it soothed her, too. She doubted her fear for a moment, thought that he might be right, that she was silly, overreacting, too sensitive. Her hands trembled when she placed her palms flat against the door as if she could feel him through the wood and paint, feel his honesty or deception, and she found that she wanted to feel honesty.

He said, "I'm leaving now. I'm sorry if I scared you."

She listened as he stepped down the first flight, and she heard floorboards creak as he turned onto the landing. She gasped for breath and left her palms on the door, and she stayed there a long time until she felt certain of his absence, and was glad for it, and missed his voice. She hadn't yet stopped crying. She began to sob and to speak as she sobbed, only half-aware of what it was she was saying. "Daddy," she gasped. "Daddy."

From the moment Suzanne sneaked their father's last note back from the trash, she had imagined him still in her life.

She had seen such things in movies. She imagined that he sold the house, then moved into an apartment in Hartford. He knew it was best he stay away but—tortured by longing—came to the schoolyard in the morning to watch her start her day. He watched her walk home. He spied on her in the park when she took Chryssie there on the days Howard and Karen wanted the apartment to themselves. He arrived at Mass after the service began and admired her from the back pew, leaving just after communion. So in church, she turned to search the back rows, and she paused in the schoolyard to study cars parked nearby, and at the park and at the grocery and even from the back porch of their apartment, she looked for him.

When in her fantasies she found him, or when he showed himself to her, she forgave him.

After the bald man left, she stayed in the house for four days. She kept the doors locked. She quit her job by not going. When she slept, she could not tell she was asleep. When she was awake, she could not tell she was awake. She ate almost nothing. She kept the television on but didn't watch. She crept once into the stairwell to retrieve her pencils and sketchbook. She tore drawings out of her sketchbook and taped them to the walls, and when she ran out of tape she stapled them and when she ran out of staples she used a hammer and nails. When she ran out of faces she drew more. She drew Karen and Howard and Chryssie. She drew her father. She drew the bald man. She drew until the tips of her pencils were nubs and then until the nubs were flat. Even then there weren't enough faces. The walls still had space.

The Liszaks weren't home, so she sat on their porch to wait. She wore a wrinkled sweatshirt and frayed jeans and open-toed clogs, and she felt cold. It was morning and cloudy and damp. The Liszaks did not keep a blanket on their porch.

She had a plan. She was a girl in a crowded theater, and there was only one seat open. She had practiced her speech. Orphan girl. Abandoned by her sister. She could keep Mrs. Liszak's husband company on those days he waited for his wife to tire of what was strange and beautiful and to come home. She would keep her money a secret. She would stay in Hartford and find her father or be found by him. So she sat on the Liszaks' porch, trying to look helpless. She hugged herself, pressed her legs together against the chill morning, and shivered, and waited.

They walked home together, Mrs. Liszak's husband carrying grocery bags. He looked surprised to see Suzanne. Mrs. Liszak did not. She unlocked the door.

"The girl's freezing," he said, and he put down the bags. "Come inside, girl."

But Mrs. Liszak touched his shoulder, turned him away. "Take the groceries to the kitchen, Charlie," she said. "I'll worry about Suzanne."

Suzanne peeked up; her plan had called for pity in Mrs. Liszak's face, but she saw only disdain. Mrs. Liszak said: "There's nothing for you here. Go away."

"Can't I—?"

But Mrs. Liszak had followed her husband and shut the door behind her.

Suzanne listened to the click of the deadbolt. Locked out of a house, locked into a life. That was it, then. No Liszaks. No Eagle Scout. No Karen. No mother. No Daddy.

She doubled over, weeping. She noticed through tears the chipped polish of her toenails poking out from her clogs, saw a carpenter's nail stick up from a floorboard, saw rust on the flat head of the nail. The nail's shaft was bent. Another nail beside it stayed driven into the dry, gray wood. She counted four nails per plank. She counted a dozen planks. Two dozen. So many nails. Nails everywhere. She felt grief everywhere. It filled the porch and the yard, the street; in comparison she grew into insignificance. She wept and watched herself shrink, helpless. Her head reeled. She felt a peculiar peace.

She would know this strange calm again, but not for years, not until two serene hours trapped alone in a broken elevator during a week of art-school exams. She would not understand this peculiar peace until she had lain in a sleeping bag in a New Hampshire mountain meadow, her fiancé snoring and the Milky Way unraveling across the sky. Years after that, she would expect to feel it (and would) in the delivery room of a California hospital as she watched Karen bring forth a second son. But now it made no sense, this thrill at her own impotence, her own triviality, not here on the Liszaks' porch, having gone too long without food, exhausted, vision blurred. Time stopped, too, and she stumbled in it, floated away from the porch, crashed into the cement walk. She felt grit in the skin of her forehead, and it didn't matter. In her mouth, she tasted blood—a tooth hung loose—and it didn't matter. The world turned upside down, then flipped back. Hands gripped her arms; hands lifted her. Someone spoke her name. Inside, the house was warm.

At the Beach

I. DOG AND NOT DOG

ROSA'S CAT WAS SHORT-HAIRED, BLACK AND WHITE, WITH HALF its left ear torn away and a tail that twitched when the cat meant to do evil. If Rosa failed to notice the tail, the cat might rake claws across her hand as she petted him. She fancied herself a cat lover, but this animal led her to thoughts of betrayal.

She enjoyed the fruits of her thirty-three years: friendships, loving parents, success in property law, and an expensive condominium in a city that valued its magnolias and crepe myrtle. People who knew her saw a woman confident in herself and her powers. She dated, but unmarried men her age proved immature or too damaged to warrant anything more than sex.

One year, in June, she left to spend a week at the beach with a KKG sister and the woman's family. This was an annual retreat, a chance for sun and talk with a friend she saw too rarely. She brought the cat along in a carrier. The house they'd rented had weathered gray and offered a view from all four bedrooms. Molly and her husband took one, put their children in another and Rosa in the third. Her bed was too soft, and she lay in it restlessly, listening through the air ducts to the kids tease each other. The fourth bedroom they gave to a friend of the husband's. The friend owned small-circulation regional magazines Rosa had read in boutiques. He was a transplanted Yankee and, as Molly had promised, single.

"Married once," he said. "College sweethearts. We both learned things."

Also, he'd brought a dog.

Later his dog met her cat, and it was a day before the cat would come out from under the house. It clawed her when she finally pulled it into her arms, left hot little lines, the blood beading atop the cuts.

None of this made him memorable. She had met single Yankee men before. Some even had dogs. What struck her about him (what would strike anyone) were the scars that marked his arms and legs, chest and back. The jigsaw patterns changed color in different light. In some places his body hair grew out of his scarred skin as it would on any other man, and in other places—where, perhaps, the scars were deeper?—his skin looked papery and bald. The resulting impression was of a man unfinished. Molly had whispered the cause to her when the Yankee was off fishing: a bad fire when he was a boy. Molly believed everyone had a soft spot for wounds.

He apologized for his dog and after that took greater care when she or her cat was nearby. He befriended the cat, which crawled on his lap when he sat on the porch, the two of them fixated on the yellow-blue horizon. The cat never clawed him.

One afternoon Molly sent Rosa and the Yankee to fetch groceries. Molly could wink without moving her eyes.

The dog rode in the backseat. Rosa, looking out the window at the dunes and high grasses, absently caressed the scratches on her arm and asked about his magazines. She felt comfortable with his driving, which was fast, easy, confident. She had never ridden in a BMW. She liked the sting of salt in the ocean air and the rumble of the tires on the road. At the grocery, before they released their seat belts, she noticed vending machines at some distance on the store's concrete apron. Sunlight gleamed off the glass-and-metal fronts of the machines, one of which sold pop and cola. She couldn't say with certainty what the other advertised. She knew what it appeared to offer, and the idea charmed her.

"I'm crazy," she said, "but I believe that vending machine sells Blind Faith."

He looked.

"Maybe," he said. "What comes out of a Blind Faith machine?"

"Probably blind faith."

"In a can? In a wrapper?"

She said, "What faith would you pick? Faith in Allah? Jesus? The almighty dollar?"

He said, "Blind faith must cost more than a dollar."

She said, "I'll buy." She'd been raised Southern Baptist, and though she had strayed she often felt the tug.

She jingled coins in her hand as they passed the soda machine, but there was no blind faith for sale after all, only live bait—worms and maggots—for a dollar. Inside, they filled the basket from Molly's list, and he added a pouch of dried pigs' ears for his dog.

At the beach house that night, she whistled, but the cat gave no answer. Later, as she walked sand-swept sidewalks and then to the wharf whistling for her cat, she felt God working in her life. She never saw the cat again.

II. CROAKERS

The day moved toward dusk, and the wind rose, its fiercest gusts scouring them with beach sand. She pushed her hair behind her ears, but dark strands blew loose over her face.

She explained. She said, "Rosalyn was the First Lady's name. Mine is Rosalind. Like in Shakespeare's play."

"Rosalind is difficult to say," he said. "That D."

"You have to want to say it."

He'd taken a break from fishing. He had a length of PVC pipe driven into the sand near the waterline and his fishing pole propped inside it. He was fishing for anything worth eating, but pulling in only croakers. The fish made their croaking sounds as he pried them from the barbs, tossed them underhand back into the sea, then loaded up with bait again.

She told him her age. He was forty-two.

"I work long hours," he said.

"So do I. And much of my social life is entangled with the firm. Entertaining clients and whatnot. Are you churchgoing?"

"No. I'm a lapsed Catholic."

"You're looking at a lapsed Baptist."

They each nodded and smiled. He fingered a snail shell out of the sand.

"But Sunday morning is pure to me," she said. "I don't work then."

He wore a loose sweatshirt that covered many of his scars, but he was in shorts and was barefoot. She wanted to touch the scars on his leg, to see how they felt. The shape of his legs was right and, in the case of his calves, beautiful. But the skin was all wrong. She showed him her toe that had no nail.

"I dropped a microwave oven on that when I was moving once," she said.

"Moving out or in?"

"Out."

"Was leaving him worth losing the toenail?"

"Oh yes."

He said, "There are nights I can't sleep."

"Because of the fire?"

"No. Other things."

"Does the fire matter?"

"To some folks. It was at a circus. Outdoors. A tent burned and killed a lot of people. My mother and I were there. She seldom talks about it, and I don't remember much."

"I remember the microwave oven. A gift from my parents."

He said, "My parents came from Poland before I was born. I've heard every dumb Polack joke ever told."

She said, "My family's been poor since before the Civil War. But my daddy made some big money. We're new at it. I'm sure sometimes we are crude and offensive. Just like the new-money people in Faulkner. But we don't mean it."

"I haven't read Faulkner."

"Do you have children?"

"No."

"Do you want children?"

"Yes. Do you?"

"Yes."

He checked his bait can. He'd run out. He hauled in the line, found a croaker on the end of it. He took a knife from his pocket and decapitated the croaker and dropped its head in the can. Then he sliced the belly and with a finger scooped out the tiny entrails. He spread these among the hooks, added the head to another, then cast it all back into the sea. He rinsed his hands in the salt water and returned to where she sat. He sat so as to shield her from the occasional frenzy of wind and sand. When he spoke her full name, it sounded as if the *D* came naturally.

She admired how his hands had worked the knife and the fish. She had read Faulkner and studied law and watched her father increase his fortune; from these things she understood that civilization is built and maintained through killing, and she meant to have a civilized life.

III. TURTLE

An afternoon of swimming and bodysurfing and sunbathing led the tired grown-ups to the porch and to vodka cocktails, as seagulls laughed overhead and a band played at a nearby house. Earlier that day there'd been a wedding; now the party: the bride exchanging her dress for an all-white bikini with a tiara and veil; the groom donning a black Speedo, a bow tie around his neck like a male stripper. She chased him with a paddle, laughing and slapping at his tush.

"Did you bring your bow tie?" Molly asked her husband.

"Only my body oil," he said.

Molly howled. She said to her husband, "You've got such pale skin, you get out there with body oil and a bow tie and the only thing gonna jump your bones is a penguin! You work best in the dark, honey."

Rosa refused to picture the Yankee in a bow tie and body oil. Though she had just met him, she'd begun to imagine him in her bed, and she felt it necessary to see him dignified, solemn. She did not want the scars sewn across his body to be part of some freak-show striptease.

Then the kids, back from a night hunt for sand crabs, thundered up the stairs, their flashlights waving, their voices sharp and astonished.

"There's a turtle!" the first cried. "There's a turtle on the beach!"

"A big one!"

"You can't see it 'cause it's dark!"

"It walked right up on the sand!"

"It crawled!"

"It's bigger than this!"

So the grown-ups hurried down, chasing the kids to a spot where a dozen or so people had gathered.

"Keep your distance," someone said.

"She's laying eggs," said another.

"Come up at sunset, right between my fishing pole and my buddy's there."

"Don't shine that flashlight on her!"

Rosa could not see the turtle, but she saw the turtle dig. It kicked backwards with powerful fins, tossing sand into the moonlight with great urgency. Shovelfuls sprayed through the air, and Rosa tried to imagine some backyard swamp turtle big enough to do this. She curled her toes in the sand.

"Someone ought to call the ranger," said Molly's husband. He looked around. "Might as well be me."

Rosa leaned near the Yankee. "Can you see anything?" she said.

"Just a dark lump."

The ranger, when he arrived, called the turtle a loggerhead. "Back to the beach where she was hatched," said the ranger. "That's how they do it. They'll come a thousand miles. They mate on the water's surface. The male hooks his foreclaws into the female's shoulders to get a grip. By the end, she's usually scratched and bleeding."

It was dark now, and they could only make out the spot where they knew the turtle to be and what might be a lump. People drifted away. Molly and her husband took their children home except for the oldest girl, Sara, who wanted to stay. Rosa volunteered to watch with Sara, and the Yankee said he would, too.

They stayed three hours. Sara and Rosa sat in the sand, the girl huddling for warmth against the woman's bare legs. The Yankee and the ranger stood, peering into the dark. Late in their vigil, the turtle bellowed: a guttural birthing song.

"She'll lay a hundred or more eggs," said the ranger.

Then the turtle shifted. It turned. It pushed thick mounds of sand over the nest. Rosa watched unblinking as she would through a hole in time to the days before Eden. The turtle crawled along as if it and the sand had been born of the same mother. The ranger, at a distance, kept pace. Just before the turtle reached the water, the ranger turned on his flashlight. The turtle looked orange in places, and green, and black, and her beaked head did not turn to the light. Water lapped against her, washing grainy sand from her carapace. She pulled herself deeper. The ocean lifted her. She vanished into the foam. Rosa watched, and when the turtle had gone realized that she held Sara's hand with her left and the Yankee's hand with her right.

Then the ranger pounded stakes around the nest, and the Yankee helped tie string to make a border. To the string, the ranger fastened blaze-orange tape and signs warning people away.

"I'll alert the biologists," he said. "They'll want to move these eggs someplace safer. There's a preserve to the south."

Molly and her husband greeted them from the porch with a pitcher of sea breezes. Sara told the tale, and as she spoke Rosa watched the Yankee and dreamed of the turtle. What monstrous beauties. But there was beast in her, too, and she shivered to imagine the small cruelties she and the Yankee might visit on each other's grateful selves.

IV. TURTLE EGG

In the morning she crept about the beach house, her brain swollen with vodka and squeezing against her skull, her pulse hammering the vertebrae in her neck. Over a loud, buttery breakfast, she tried to conceal her suffering. She smiled when the children told jokes, nibbled toast, accepted gratefully the aspirin Molly sneaked her. Against her better judgment, she agreed to go with everyone to the beach to see the turtle nest.

The Yankee had not kissed her the night before. On the porch they'd drunk sea breezes, and their mood became one of laughter and flirtation. They let the taste of cranberry juice and lime swirl in their mouths, dreamed of their turtle deep beneath the black waves, sucked ice cubes softened by vodka and two a.m. air. When they parted company, he pressed her hands between his, said good night, then left her wanting more.

Now she knelt beside him, hung over and pretending otherwise, part of a circle of volunteers crouched around the turtle's nest. They dug with an archaeologist's care, ever ready for the alien texture that meant another egg. Already they'd collected dozens, directed by a pretty, young government biologist come to save the unborn turtles.

The eggs didn't seem so fragile. When the biologist had lifted the first one for all to see, Rosa thought it resembled a wet Ping-Pong ball and was surprised to hold it and find heft at its core, the shell like leather, not a wafery plastic.

Ted, Rosa thought. His name. When she'd spoken it the night before, he told her that he liked how she lengthened the vowel nearly to two syllables. He was not then some typical Yankee, puffing himself up by mocking a drawl, acting as if all the world ought to be dull as the Pilgrims. No, he was a man appreciating the music only Rosa could make of his name.

Leaning over the turtle nest, he whispered, "How's your head?"

He knew. She said, "Leathery and wet."

He smiled, so she had somehow the sense that her hangover was precious to him, that hers was the world's loveliest hangover. His kind manner helped her past embarrassment and put her hungover self at ease. Maybe he'd learned that, how to put people at ease, by living with his scars. Such a skill could fend off staring, help him fit in. Why is it, she thought, that characters in movies and on TV always learn that fitting in is bad, that parading your freakishness is the bravest path, and then, in the end, that the reward for reveling in your strangeness is love? That was untrue to life. Sometimes love came because you could fit in, because you helped people feel at ease with your strangeness.

If this sense of ease was love, she'd never felt a finer one.

He leaned nearer. She could hear his breath soft at her ear.

"You can kiss it," she whispered. "My head."

She waited. She wanted him to know the things she spoke of with no one. That she ate fast-food burgers to celebrate paydays; that she still believed in God and prayed to Jesus; that one awful rush night she and the others forced a Kappa pledge to dance naked before football players until the girl wept; that she sends the girl flowers every year on her birthday. If he kissed her hungover head, he could share these secrets. With his kiss, she believed, he could ease her through tomorrow and every day after, through all unexplored things, even his own strange embrace.

The biologist, who was a few months out of graduate school, watched him kiss her and thought: That's what it's like to have loved for years.

Elephant

I WAS THIRTEEN WHEN MY FATHER TOLD ME HE ONCE SHOT A CIR-
cus elephant.

"Through the eye," he said.

We sat in the dim light of Gray's Tavern. It was payday, and on
most paydays we killed afternoons at Gray's. My father chased vodka
with Knickerbocker beer, and smoked his Marlboros. I sipped cola
from a glass bottle.

"With a Colt .45, semi-automatic," he said. "Civilian issue. A tiny
gun for such a big animal."

My father is dead now. Emphysema. He'd smoked since he was a
boy in southeastern Poland, hauling lumber out of the woods, which
was a dangerous job. Africa and Italy during the war were dangerous,
too, but what eventually got him were the two packs a day. He enjoyed
cigarettes, and he enjoyed his factory job. He loved my mother.

"I love her more than God loves her," he once said, as we sat around
the dinner table eating stuffed cabbage and meatloaf.

Mama frowned and said, "Your papa is a simple man."

When she spoke that truth—and she spoke it often—she was describing the man who rocked in a chair on our front porch, listening as the Yankees played at 1080 on the AM dial, tossing bits of stale
pumpernickel bread to blue jays and starlings and calling them sweet
names. "I'm out to feed my chickens," he would say as he stepped onto

the porch, and the birds would swoop to our yard from neighborhood rooftops and branches. This was Mama's simple man.

Mama wanted not to be simple. She kept secrets. She spent afternoons alone in her sewing room with the door closed. Sometimes at Sunday Mass she cried but would never say why. My friends and the parents of my friends talked about her. My mother cleaned houses, but she should have been an actress. From her I learned that the redeeming currency of old pain is drama.

Our family's pain is old enough. Not long after my father left for the war, there was a fire in Hartford that killed nearly two hundred people. The fire is famous not so much for the horrific deaths it caused, but for where they occurred. A circus tent burned that afternoon. No one knows for sure how the fire started, but it consumed the tent so quickly that the crowds inside were trapped. Flaps of flaming canvas fell from the sky. There was black smoke. Panic. Screaming circus animals. A famous photograph shows Emmett Kelly, the saddest of clowns, carrying a water bucket, which, given the scale of black-and-white ruin around him, holds nothing but its own inadequacy. His hobo pants are shredded and his hand bats the air, obscuring his face so all you can see is his bulbous nose and his frown. My mother and I went to the circus for that matinee. We spent weeks in St. Francis Hospital after. Her scars included half a butterfly on her forehead that she never attempted to hide. Mine cover much of my body, but not my face or hands. People who see my scars ask how I got them, and then they ask what it was like to be inside the tent. They are always disappointed when I admit that I can't remember. In truth, I'm disappointed, too. When I asked about the fire, my mother would only say I was blessed to have forgotten. She saw no reason to interfere with God's plan for my memory.

I remember Gray's Tavern, though. It's still there: a little hole in the sidewalk down Maple Avenue near Goodwin Park. It's an Irish bar, and I think my father liked it because he felt supremely Polish there. Surrounded by all the Gavins and Carraghers and Bolgers, his difference shone—the whisper of his Slavic accent, his Slavic eyebrows, his flat, round face. Each time we walked through the door the bartender and proprietor—Eddie Gray, who served with my father in Italy—greeted Papa with the opening line of a joke.

"Hey Charlie, how many Polacks does it take to tie a shoe?"

"Hey Charlie, did you hear about the Polack and the cabaret singer?"

"Hey Charlie, what's the difference between a Polack and a platypus?"

"Zip the lip, Mick," my father would say, and Eddie Gray would laugh and so would anyone else in the bar. It was their way of saying hello, how the hell are you, it's good to see you and we love you, you Polack son-of-a-peasant. Come have a drink.

Behind the bar, a baseball trophy: "Gray's Tavern, Twilight League Runners-up, 1948." Their best season ever. Eddie Gray throwing strikes from the mound one game and stabbing line drives at short the next. A year later his arm went bum, and without him the Grays couldn't even beat Traveler's Insurance. In the corner of the tavern, a map of "Irlande" hung from the wall, and superimposed over it was a shirted man with his collar open and a rifle in his hand. Below him, the clarion whoop, "They may kill the revolutionary, but they will never kill the Revolution." Jimmy Williams always sat beside the poster. Jimmy, who was not so old but had the pleading, helpless eyes of a spaniel, and who fingered tunes and hymns on a recorder for coins. "Danny Boy," of course. But also "When You Wish upon a Star" and each version of the memorial acclamation of the Roman Catholic Mass, proclaiming the mysteries of faith. Only slow tunes, and each note arrived on the air weak in the knees, as if Jimmy first had to think before letting it go. Papa used to tell me not to stare at Jimmy. He always gave Jimmy a dollar.

This was 1954, ten years after the fire.

It was the wet early April of that year when I heard about the elephant. The thermometer said it wasn't cold, but the wind and the spit-

ting rain gave the air a bite. My nose stung and dripped. Papa waited
for me outside the school gate. He never liked for me to walk anywhere alone.

When I drew within range, he spread his arms and scooped me
into them. He cupped my head and kissed my brow with cold lips.
Without a word, we splashed through puddles to Gray's.

At the bar, a man with grease-blackened hands and a bandage on
his forefinger was introducing himself and a friend to Eddie. "This is
Brendan, my birthday buddy," said the man, and he lit a cigarette. "We
got the same birthday, and it's today."

"Charlie," Eddie shouted to my father, "how do you sink a Polack
battleship?"

"Same as a Mick ship. You put it in water."

"Have I tried that one before?"

"A year ago February."

Eddie slid the vodka and the beer across the bar, and the fizzing
cola for me. Papa and I sat at our regular table, which tilted my way
if he lifted his elbows. He sipped his vodka, his smiles lasting only a
moment. He swirled the glass so ice sang on the edges, then sipped
again. I still try to remember whether he chewed his lip or blinked too
much or suffered from some twitch that, had I been paying attention,
would have shown me that my father was not himself that day. Nothing comes to mind. I wasn't paying attention to him. Not yet. It was a
payday afternoon at Gray's, like so many others.

"Do kids tease you still?" he said.

"Sometimes they want to touch my skin," I said. "I don't mind."

In the corner, Jimmy Williams played his recorder, each note
squeezed to life.

When

you

wish

u-

pon

a

"In Italy," my father said to me, "I had POW duty. You know what that is, POW? Prisoners of war."

He rapped his knuckles three times on our table. Eddie brought him another round.

"I was like a guard in a jail," Papa said. "It was easy most of the time. But we had one fascist—solid-as-bone that guy—kept yelling at us, 'Goddamn GIs. Bastard GIs. Goddamn GIs.'"

My father never swore when I was around. Yet now he spoke forbidden words casually, as if they had no power. But they did. Dark, gristly power. I leaned nearer.

"He had a mouth, that guy," my father said. "Over and over. Like a mynah bird. The kind of thing that would drive you crazy, like someone on a Saturday morning trying to start a car, turning over the engine six, seven, eight times. 'Goddamn GI. Bastard GI.' This fascist, he's on us like that until this one fella, this one fella, he picks up a chunk of brick from a bombed-out building, and he breaks all that fascist's teeth. Bashed him right across the chops. That son-of-a-gun kept on, though: 'Goddamn GI. Bastard GI.' Grinning at us with his mouth and tongue swollen. Blood all over his lips. I watched, wishing he'd zip it, you know? Because he was stupid, because all that happened was he got smashed in the mouth again, then again. I hated him for that. Now, I don't know. Now he's just a fact of life."

Brendan's birthday buddy at the bar was explaining his bandaged finger, how he'd cut it to the bone at the typewriter factory where he worked. He offered to show Eddie the stitches. I had stitches in my chin when I was eight after falling from my bicycle, and of course I knew all about scars from flame. But I had never seen a man whose mouth was shredded by a brick. I ran my tongue over the fronts of my top teeth between the gum and the lip. I imagined my mouth like the stringy inside of a pumpkin, all bloody. Street water from the rubbers covering my shoes pooled with the grime under my chair.

"I read about the fire in an army newspaper," my father said. He wouldn't let go of his vodka glass. Now he tapped its bottom against the table. "But I didn't worry. Your mama and me, we didn't have much money, not enough to spend on circus tickets. I read about the fire, and I wrote your mother a letter. I asked if we knew anyone who had been there."

He shook a cigarette from his pack, but didn't light it. He took off his eyeglasses and chuckled, but the sound was small and sad. He rubbed his eyes and then the bridge between them. My father had deep indentations in his nose because the lenses of his glasses weighed so much. When Papa died, Mr. Kowalczyk at the mortuary suggested masking the indentations with makeup, but I said leave them and have Papa wear his glasses instead.

"There was a fella. A PFC from Waterbury. We never talked much, but his sister had gone to the circus. She'd been burned, though not bad enough for him to get compassion leave. Not like your mother and you were burned. I didn't know what happened to you yet. I just knew about this fella's sister. So I bought him a beer. Patted his shoulder. He showed everybody her picture. She was eighteen. Good-looking. A lot of the fellas made jokes about her afterward because she was so pretty." Papa looked at me suddenly, as if remembering who sat across from him. "You don't make jokes about pretty girls, do you?" he said. "You and the other boys at school? Your mother was a pretty girl. Never make jokes about pretty girls."

I nodded that I wouldn't.

"Your mother's not a girl anymore," he said.

He loved her. I believe this. Yet many times I woke to find Papa on the couch downstairs. "I snore," he told me. "Keeps your mama awake." His answer never sounded whole. Nor did my mother's, when I asked why I had no brother or sister. She would kiss my nose and whisper, "God gave us one perfect child."

Brendan's birthday buddy tossed peanuts into the air and caught them in his mouth. He suggested Eddie buy a pinball machine to add some whiz-bang to the place. "Whiz-bang's out that door," Eddie said. "We like peace and quiet in here."

Papa lit his Marlboro and shook out the match. He hadn't looked away from me.

"How was I supposed to know how badly you were hurt?" he said. "I don't . . . Jesus. I'm in Italy. A goddamned bastard GI. It took a while for the nurses to get your names. Your mama's English wasn't so good then. You . . . I hate to think it. About a week after I read about the fire—must have been more than a week later—a Red Cross woman took me aside. She held my hand. She told me."

The army sent my father home. He arrived on a hot, hazy afternoon, stepping out of the Union Station into a city that seemed to him strangely serene. No mortar fire. No screams. No bombed-out buildings. "Queer" is how he described it that day in Gray's Tavern.

Now when I imagine my father home that first hour, I imagine him walking through the working streets of downtown, amid secretaries and switchboard operators, lawyers and bookkeepers. He pauses at the corner of Trumbull and Pearl to take in the old Hartford Insurance Company building, the stone stag over its door. His khaki uniform is crisp, and he squints into the stark July sun at the building's cornices and windowpanes that stand intact. An Italian man in a white T-shirt tries to sell him a newspaper. My father breathes cologne and perfume. Women smell clean. It's a good day to live. It makes no sense. An ocean away is a fascist with his mouth stuffed full of blood-soaked cotton, and my father understands why. But here in this familiar and alien place, this place so at peace it seems not of the world, his wife and son lie alone in hospital beds, their skin peeled. He is home, and he staggers at the horror.

Years later at Gray's, my father stared at the grain of our tabletop and traced a knot with his hard, thick thumbnail.

"I didn't visit you for three days," he said. "I stayed away for three days."

Then he looked at me as if I would accuse him, as if a thirteen-year-old, knowing only the sting of cola on his tongue and the smell of stale beer and cigarettes, could pass judgment. I was too young to understand what three days meant. All I understood was that my father was tattling on himself, confessing something that made him seem small.

He told me of those three days.

First he returned to the apartment. It was mostly as he remembered, though my mother's jade plant sat root-bound in its pot, and the landlord had painted the windows black in case of air raids. In the room where I had slept, my father opened dresser drawers and lifted out shirts and jumpers and shoes that were too large for the baby he remembered, and—having been gone those two years—he could not imagine the boy who might fit into them. Instead he turned his hand to chores. He swept and mopped the floor, then dusted window-sills and the small shrine my mother had built to the Virgin Mary. He watered the victory garden she had planted in the backyard and had marked with a small penciled sign that read "Ania Liszak" to distinguish it from other tenants' gardens. He changed a washer in the bathroom faucet to stop a drip, and he patched a torn window screen. He moved from chore to chore as if everything hinged on his labor. Still, he failed. He dropped a light bulb and it shattered. He knocked over an end table and left a gash in the floor. He worked past dark, past midnight, until he couldn't help but sleep, leaning in the corner where he had yet to finish mending a crack in the plaster. Not until the next morning would he dare step into their bedroom to run his fingers along the sheets where she had slept, to smell her pillow, to touch the hair still twined in her brush.

On the second day he shopped, telling himself he couldn't visit the hospital empty-handed. He took most of the morning and all of the afternoon to find just the right gifts, wandering shop to store in awe and confusion. He discovered that time and distance had made him uncertain of what his wife and son would most want. Would his boy play that board game? Could he look through that magnifying glass? Would she wear such a fancy blouse? He settled on a box of colored pencils for me; for Mama he chose a frame for a family photograph. To wrap these gifts, he bought silver paper and red ribbon.

Though he wasn't hungry, he forced himself to stop at the downtown five-and-dime where he sat on a swivel stool at the counter. He ordered a root beer and fried egg sandwich. As he ate, he overheard in the booth behind him a woman in a flowered hat talking to a friend. She was talking about the circus. He listened more closely. The woman in the flowered hat told her friend that most of the circus was still in Hartford—right up there on Barbour Street. Yes, the circus! It can't leave, she said. There are so many lawsuits already, and no one knows how the circus will pay. Gorillas and lions as collateral, she laughed. It's true! All the animals survived! I read it in the *Times*. Not a singed whisker. Why, they've even got elephants in Sponzo's Meadow!

My father left his root beer and a few coins on the counter. He walked out to the sidewalk, surprised by the bright sun. That night at the apartment, he drank too much beer. And then he lay awake imagining me and my mother sitting in the grandstands as fire flashed around us, the animals outside and safe from the flames, and because he did not know the neighborhood a few miles north where the circus tent had burned, he saw instead a war-wrecked Italian countryside where elephants and lions stepped softly through the dust. Twice he left his bed to vomit, but his stomach was empty and the heaves brought no relief.

On his third day home, Papa caught a bus downtown and another north on Main Street. From there, he walked.

The smell struck him first, carried by wind. The smell of dry, sweet ash mixed with animal stink, rich and nauseating, and Papa spit but couldn't get it out of his mouth. Then he came to the field where the big top had burned.

"It was like an army camp," he told me. "Except it was like the sloppy camp of troops who'd been beaten. Tents with walls flapping loose—not a proper tie-down to be found."

He stubbed the butt of his cigarette in one of Eddie Gray's foil ashtrays.

There were trucks, he told me, parked and rusted and caked with mud. Railroad cars painted red, though the paint had bubbled and split, the fire had been so hot. One car smelled like the kitchen, and another was obviously the latrine. Rough characters lounged all over, their shirts unbuttoned and untucked, their T-shirts stained yellow under the arms. Only a few of them worked, carrying hay by the arm-ful for the animals.

"Gorillas. Lions," my father said. "Amazing, yes. But I'd seen goril-las and lions at zoos in cages, and this wasn't so different. But I'd never seen an elephant. Only in picture books."

He lit another cigarette, letting the smoke ease out of his nostrils before he spoke again.

"These elephants they kept staked and crowded into a meadow, with just a man or two to watch them. You could hardly see the stakes, and it didn't take much to imagine the elephants running from the lot, trampling a bunch of neighborhood kids playing stickball. But all the elephants did was stuff their trunks into these banged-up barrels full of water and sometimes drink and other times spray themselves like they were their own garden hose. Geez, it was hot. My shirt stuck to my back. I found a shade tree, but it didn't help. Shade didn't help.

"The elephants were all the same color—like ash," he said. His eyes grew wet, and he blinked, his voice quiet as if steadied by certainty. "And they were giants. Bigger than the piles of hay. And those piles were as big as cars. Mountains of hay in front of them, mountains of shit behind them. The stink would make you dizzy. Flies, too, zig-zagging near your ears, your eyes. All you could hear was that buzz-ing. Louder, then quiet; louder, then quiet. And then those elephants would sound off. Raise their heads, their trunks, then blast away. Even on a day hot as that, it'd turn your spine cold."

Papa told me that he walked around the meadow a dozen or more times, waving off flies and eyeing the elephants. He drew close enough to study where their pigmentation spotted and the flesh became pink or dull white. "Like they had been burned," he said. "But they hadn't." He wagged a finger. "You had, though. You had. I tell you, Teddy, they seemed like something born when the mountains came up from the oceans. Something that survived everything."

Papa drew close to the elephants, so close that he could see even the bristle of hairs along the bottom of a jaw, the stunted tusks hidden inside an elephant mouth, the depression above and behind an eye.

"But over there was a block full of three-family houses, one with a porch swing. And power poles up and down the street, their lines running from house to house. And there, a '41 Oldsmobile. Sheets hung out to dry. It didn't make any sense." His eyes sparkled with the monstrousness of it. His voice grew loud. "Those elephants, you know, they were just wrong. There weren't supposed to be elephants in meadows in Hartford. Everything was wrong. Every last thing was wrong."

I glanced to Eddie Gray, who wiped the bar with a caramel-colored rag. He saw me—it was plain on his face—but he turned aside, started working down the other way.

My father grabbed my arm and hissed, "Look at me when I'm talking to you."

"Yes."

"Do you understand? Their stink would peel paint. The inside of my nose was burning."

He pinched his nose. When he let go, the skin was pink.

Jimmy had stopped playing his recorder. The bar seemed too quiet, as if everyone were listening. But I didn't dare turn to look.

"You understand, Teddy? These were elephants right here in Hartford. Lounging in a meadow as if this is the way the world is supposed to be. But it's not. It's not. So I shot one. I walked up close to the elephant at the end of the row, away from the circus workers. It was so easy. So slow. Its head swung toward me. I fired right into its eye."

He reared as if I would challenge him.

"There was blood," he said. "Elephant blood on my uniform."

Now Eddie approached our table.

"Hey, Charlie, maybe it's time you headed home, huh?"

"I'm talking to my son," Papa said. "I'm explaining things."

Eddie snorted. He took the empty glasses, wiped our table and left the smell of dishrags.

"Did the elephant die?" I asked.

"Maybe," my father said. "I'm not proud to have shot an elephant.

I'm telling you that everything was wrong, and that all I could do was shoot the elephant. And then I ran. I'm not proud of that, either, Teddy. I ran."

I nodded.

"It was a Colt .45, semi-automatic," he said. "I think the elephant would have been blinded, but not killed. No, not killed."

I nodded.

"They're big animals," he said.

Eddie came back with another cola.

"Here, kid. On the house."

My father acted as if he didn't notice. "Time to go," he said.

In less than an afternoon, my father had become new, different, strange. I wasn't yet ready to be alone with him. I pointed to the full bottle. "I haven't finished my soda," I said.

"Drink fast."

He stood and walked back to the toilet, his steps sure and deliberate, leaving me alone, heavy with responsibility and adolescent grief because he had shot the elephant on my behalf. Because of an injury I couldn't even remember, an elephant had been blinded.

Brendan's birthday buddy said something then, about the tears and soft lips of a sad woman. "That's what I want for my birthday," he said. He swiveled on his stool to face me. "Kid," he said, "never forget that a crying woman is a beautiful thing."

Papa and I walked home through a dark drizzle. Headlights rushed past, and gutter water splashed over the curb to the sidewalks. When we got home he turned on the radio, then sat in his rocking chair and wiped his glasses clean for a long time.

He never again spoke to me of the elephant he had shot. When I tried to bring it up, he changed the subject. Eventually he did tell me of his first visit to see us in the hospital, how I protested that no, this stranger was not my papa, until a nurse vouched for him. But the nurses wouldn't let him touch me and wouldn't let him give me the colored pencils. Neither my father nor the pencils were sterile. My mother, my father told me, wept when she saw the family portrait in its wood frame painted gold. When he told me this, it had been years since we'd spent afternoons at Gray's Tavern. I saw an opportunity and asked why he took so long to visit. He shrugged and said, "All I know is that I love you and your mother more than God loves you, because He burned you, and I'd never do that."

Time passed. My sorrow for the elephant disappeared with my pimples. I graduated high school, studied business in college, and I learned to embrace the elephant story as I would a favorite gift. Now and again I'd pull it out, turn it over, admire it, enjoy pride in owning it. Who else could claim such a thing? I couldn't remember my own circus fire story, so I would tell my father's. I'd reveal it to friends late at night after too many shots of bourbon made my tongue dry and loose. I shared the story with women in hopes that my escape from the tent combined with my father's dangerous history would impress them. Oftentimes it did.

But there was my first wife who asked, "If the gun was civilian issue, where did he get it?" I couldn't say. He never kept guns in the house. She peppered her salad, said, "I'm surprised he wasn't hurt. You'd think the elephant would have gone crazy and him standing right next to it. It might have trampled him or grabbed him with its trunk and smashed him against the ground."

"Maybe it couldn't see him," I said. We both shrugged. She asked, "When he went to have his uniform cleaned, wouldn't someone have asked how he got all that blood on it?" and "Aren't you angry that he left you in the hospital bed for three days?" She was a persistent, questioning woman who challenged everything and accepted nothing, and maybe that's why we're no longer together. But her questions made me wonder about the story my father had told me on that brittle afternoon in Gray's Tavern. I believed him, but I doubted his story.

In the basement of the Connecticut State Library there are thousands of documents that tell the story of the circus fire. Letters, photographs, government reports on onionskin paper copied with carbon. I spent days there turning fragile page after fragile page. I suffered headaches and nausea from spinning microfilm. My father's story had brought me into the library, but I let myself lose him in the larger history of the fire. This was as close as I had ever come to knowing the world in which I burned and later became patched together by skin grafts. In the end, though, even what the library held was not enough. It was cold and lacked life. So I turned back to my father's story, which felt closer to my own truth than any government record.

I learned that the circus did remain in Hartford with its elephants—but it rolled out of town on the railroad ten days after the fire. If it is true that my father left Italy more than a week after reading the news, traveled across an ocean, then spent two days in Hartford before visiting the circus grounds, how could he have made it in time to see the elephants? Perhaps my memory is faulty, or his was, and he left Italy earlier than he remembered. But I never found an account in any newspaper of an elephant being shot. Nor could I find any such report in police records.

I asked my mother once. It was a slushy winter day, and we sat in the living room drinking tea and eating kryszczyki—a fried confection powdered with sugar; "To remind us how beautiful is snow," Mama said. She had retired from cleaning houses, but Papa still worked, and he was at the factory that day. I asked about the circus elephant. She smiled as if pleased and surprised. "No, of course not," she said. When I told her the story, she laughed. "What magic! I wish he had told me."

Now I wonder about everything. Or, more accurately, I work to decide which parts of Papa's story are true. Because some of it is. I add to the story, and I subtract. Some days I believe he lied to distract from his failing: the three days he let us linger. On more generous days I put him at the circus grounds, weeping beneath a shade tree because all he sees is an empty field, and how could a tired meadow have caused his family such pain? Some days I set him in Italy, and I put a bloodied brick in his hand. Other days I bury the fascist in a grave, and I imagine a hole in his skull, opposite the eye socket.

My parents came together in the age of marriage and not in the age of divorce, and so they lived. I believe she came to love him—I saw hand-holding and gentle smiles as they aged—though how they survived those years before I don't know. I think she never wanted to love a simple man, and he knew that. Perhaps in telling me his story, he tried on the cloak of mystery and found it didn't fit, even if it was true. But he was patient, and when my mother's love eventually embraced him, it was not a love of bodies or of mystery. It's naive to think my telling the elephant story made any difference to my mother. It seems more likely that her love grew from need and proximity and time's slow unfolding.

My mother died a little over a year ago. She slipped on ice outside DiPietro's Market and afterward complained of back pain. The doctor gave her muscle relaxants, and we waited for her to feel better, not knowing an aneurysm had torn a hole in an artery. When she died, my father's depression was acute, and because he was already crippled by the emphysema, I had no choice but to move him into a nursing home. I asked him to move to North Carolina where I lived, remarried and with a son and daughter of my own, but he wouldn't leave Connecticut. "Whose games will I get?" he asked. "The Braves? That's the National League!"

A mediplex in Rocky Hill was as sane a place as I could find in Greater Hartford, but pastel prints of flowers and a jukebox in the game room couldn't disguise the small unbearable ways in which residents conceded their lives. Because of broken vertebrae, Papa's roommate shrieked with every simple shift in his bed. A woman in a wheelchair stopped most afternoons at the door of their room to curse my father and accuse him of adultery. And the Yankees seemed to lose every day.

He called me one evening last summer to ask that I come home. I had not seen him for three months. He could barely summon breath enough to speak. In words interrupted by coughing fits, he told me to fly to Connecticut right away. He told me wouldn't last past the next night.

But the doctors had said Papa would live another few months at least. And I already had a plane ticket that would bring me home in a week and a half.

"You're not dying yet," I said. "I'll be there in nine days."

"Too late," he said. "Too late."

I told him I couldn't arrange for the time off. I insisted that he wasn't dying the next day. I told him it would cost too much to re-schedule the plane ticket.

Those excuses hung on the line.

"All right," he said, and he coughed awhile.

"Good night," he said. Then he hung up.

Here is the real reason I did not go home when he called me. I was afraid. I did not want to see my father deformed and grotesque among all those others who were deformed and grotesque. I did not want to see him bloated from the steroids, wheezing through an oxygen mask, the purple capillaries in his face mapping age and pain. I was afraid to see him as a body on the verge. I was afraid to see him when he was not my father. I would visit in nine days. It would take that long to muster the courage.

The sins of the father become the sins of the son. My father did die the next day, just like he said he would. In a fluorescent-bright room, with a pitcher for his urine on the stainless steel tray beside his bed, my father tried to suck life into his lungs and life refused him. At the moment of his death I was driving along a beach in North Carolina, replaying in my head the latest disaster at work, taking for granted the pretty girls stepping out of the ocean.

Papa was buried beside Mama at St. Joseph Cemetery. Rain threat-ened, but never fell. The reception was held at Gray's Tavern. Eddie Gray has retired to Florida, and he won't fly, so he missed it, but his nephew Tom opened the doors. It's the same bar in a lot of ways, ex-cept now there's a television with cable mounted on the wall over where Jimmy Williams used to sit. Tom Gray likes the financial news, and he left the TV on with the volume muted during the reception. I followed my wife and daughter through the door, walking with my seven-year-old son and holding his hand. I'd wanted him with me, but he was still too young to appreciate the place. He and my daughter soon became bored, so I kissed them and my wife and gave them directions to a drugstore with a soda fountain.

Some of the workers from the mediplex came to the reception, and a few old men who said they knew my father, and a woman with red hair who said my parents had once been kind to her. I recognized some names, but except for Father Harvey, I received condolences from a group of strangers. When the older ones finished shaking my hand, they retreated, backs bent, to other tables. They whispered then, and I overheard as they recalled my father's ailments and the ailments of others—bleeding ulcers, ruptured spleens, tumors in the testicles.

I wish I could say that my grief got the better of me that afternoon and that in a rage against how the world is not supposed to be, I smashed the face of a drunk with a brick, or that I shot a bullet through that television screen. I did neither. Mine was the dull sorrow of a grown son, not the agony of a young father. Instead I listened to the old men talk of prostates and bile, their voices sounding distant almost to absence, and I wondered about my father in the mediplex that day when he hung up the phone and let his head fall to the pillow knowing that I had refused him and that he would die alone. Did he trust that this end was just? I worry that he did. The sins of the sons too often punish the fathers.

It was a short afternoon. Toward the end two laughing young women walked in, their skin tanned, hair bleached, and voices aged by cigarettes. They shouted out drink orders before Tom Gray could let them know they'd stumbled into a funeral reception. Then each of them hugged me and told me how sorry she was, and they asked about my father. I told them he had been a poor logger in Poland and a Polack factory worker in America. I would have told them more, but the shorter one squeezed my hand, and the blonder one stood and wished me well. They left me there, at my very small table, and finished their drinks at the bar, now leaning away from each other, now leaning near, whispering, their quiet laughter cutting through the cigarette smoke that swirled high and silver in the tavern's dull light. I wanted them to stay, to laugh louder, and when I noticed the shorter one set down her empty glass and stub out the butt of her cigarette, I signaled Tom to bring them another round on me.

Boxing Snowmen

When had it snowed?

Nick couldn't remember, a frustrating failure because clearly here was snow: days old, disheveled, wrecked by the footprints of children, newspaper carriers, and dogs, kicked about and melted in patches, not all gone but not quite there either. Sloppy, Nick thought. An unforgivable mess.

His memory, the same. How was it he could recall hurtling down the sledding hill at Goodwin Park when the kids were young, could remember the bark of metal on concrete as he shoveled those very sidewalks—the ones right there!—on an unearthly silent New Year's morning in 1971, but from nowhere in his befogged brain could he recollect this snow's arrival? If he hadn't first peered through a window just now, he'd have hobbled from the house without his galoshes.

The sedan streamed pale exhaust into the dark morning, its engine ticking in the cold. These days Lena only let him back the car out of the garage, and with that accomplished he now waited while she locked the house and made her way from the back door up the flagstone walk. "Get in the car, honey, before you freeze," she said, taking her place behind the wheel and atop the three extra cushions that allowed her to see over the dash. "And watch you don't slip."

"It's not that cold," he said.

At the grocery store she selected a cart and had him push it a few feet while she watched the wheels to make certain none was lazy. She motioned to him in a way he understood meant this cart met her approval, so he pushed while she, with hand gripping the front right corner, steered them toward a red-tag markdown on ricotta in Aisle 17.

"Cannoli for my birthday?" he asked.

"Don't be silly. You don't get desserts. It's for Franco, if he makes it. If they don't close the airport."

"Why would they close the airport?" he asked, though he sensed that answering would upset her.

"The blizzard, remember?" she said, her tone packed with the exasperation he had expected. "They said so on the news last night."

"Sure," he said, lying because he saw only a dark spot where last night should have been.

Every checkout line was clogged with old people buying in a race against the coming storm. As Nick and Lena waited, she double-checked her list: shredded wheat, grapefruit, zucchini, bottles of vitamins. "I forgot yogurt," she said. "You stay here."

When the cashier started to unload their cart, Nick watched for his wife, then snatched a package of peanut butter cups from the rack and showed it to the cashier, who was dark and pretty, maybe Puerto Rican, with green eye makeup that shimmered. He said, "We'll take this, too." Ripping the wrapper with his teeth, he shoved both cups into his mouth, then tucked the discards beneath the candy rack. The cashier grinned at him as if he were cute as the dickens. "Please," he said, lifting a fist over his mouth to hide his chewing as he spoke. "Don't look at me that way. I'm seventy-four, for God's sake."

During the drive home, traffic slowed as snow started to fall. Their car's windshield wipers chopped side to side, erasing the flakes before they could melt on the glass, leaving it cleaner, it seemed, than even the air. Nick admired the wipers' good work.

★　★　★

As he helped put away the groceries, a jar of blackberry jam fell from his hand and shattered on the floor, glass and goo everywhere.

"Now look what you've done," she said, scooting beside him, using her small body to angle him out of the way.

"The thing slipped," he said.

She stooped to pick up the larger shards. Another task. She had lived a lifetime of tasks. Days spent caring for her father, for her brother, for her children, for her husband. One after another. Laundering a kerchief into which Daddy coughed blood. Helping Gal down steps when his crippled leg was weakest. Changing diapers for Franco, ironing skirts for Denise. Now Nick, and cleaning up shattered glass and sticky jam and a thousand thousand other jobs. Lena had long ago begun imagining herself as a woman made of iron rods and pistons, a machine moving from chore to chore without rest. No time for complaint. No room for weakness. So now she ignored the damp, sorrowful fluttering in her chest and with a wet rag erased this evidence of her husband's frailty. "It slipped," she said. "But I have to clean it now. You go. Go read before you cut yourself and make me fetch bandages from the medicine cabinet."

He retreated to his recliner in the living room where the radiator knocked and the newspaper waited. Even his hands failed him now. If he had ever loved any part of his body it was his hands. He held them out so he could look at the palms, study the scaly skin and the veins and hairs as if they might show mercy and explain to him this weakness. He made a fist of one and punched it into the other's palm.

With his magnifying glass Nick skimmed headlines about the coming blizzard, snow to bury the state, winds reaching forty miles per hour, and freezing rain after dark. Turning to the sports page he read about that big heavyweight fight out in Vegas. He checked the TV listings—pay-per-view!—and clapped his hands. He remembered! He remembered talking to Franco, and he remembered Franco's promise that for Nick's birthday they'd go to the club to watch the fight. How long had it been since he sat with the fellas at the bar, elbows on the dark wood rail as he chowed on Italian sausages fried with peppers and onions, and the young guys found him through cigar smoke and laughter to ask for pointers on the jab, the feint, the flurry? Too long. A good kid, Franco, giving his father such a thoughtful birthday present.

"Not that it'll be much of a fight," he grumbled aloud.

He never understood the allure of heavyweights. Two trucks slamming into each other, and who wanted to watch that wreckage? Where was the skill? Where was the sport? From the end table he picked up a photograph clipped and framed by Lena from a newspaper some fifty years before. He read the caption though he'd read it a thousand times: "Nick DiFiore of Hartford—Welterweight State Champ." And there he stood, yellowing forever on ancient newsprint, a skinny kid lifting lollipop arms in the air, the gloves looking like a clown's, like even for boxing they were two sizes too big. But that's what got him by, those hands big as a butcher's. He had speed, too, and height and reach. All those things. But not power, no. Tommy Duncan, now he had power. But Tommy had hardly touched Nick. A few hard shots to the body, nothing crippling. Tommy was New Britain tough—a line worker from the tool factory with arms like steel cords. But Nick knew how to work him, flashing jabs at the head, looking for when Tommy cocked that right shoulder for the roundhouse, then stepping away, leaving Tommy off balance and helpless to stop Nick's counterpunches. Smart fighting. Skillful fighting. And in the ninth round Tommy quit. Just stayed in his corner. Gave the belt away. In the newspaper photograph Tommy Duncan is looking sleepy and glum while Nick DiFiore raises his stringy arms, laughing like an ape . . .

That had been a good fight. One of the last ones, too. Not long after, he decided Lena was right: Boxing wasn't the way to raise a family, not in those days. But even after he quit, even after Franco and Denise, he still relished the kind of bout when somebody was so much better by skill and by practice that what was left of the other man was different, changed forever. That was a first-rate sort of destruction, a high-quality beating, and he looked for it outside the ring, too. Back in '90, Nick had gone downtown when they imploded an insurance company tower so he could watch twenty-plus stories collapse as if into a bottomless crater because somebody knew all the right spots for the explosives.

"Hey!" he yelled toward the kitchen. "Franco's taking me to watch tonight's fight!" But even as the last word left his mouth Lena appeared, grocery receipt in hand, a look on her face to sour fresh milk.

"Why do you do this to me? This sneaking! What, you want to kill yourself?"

Nick folded his big hands, put them in his lap and looked at them as if they could help. "One candy bar won't hurt," he said. "What time is Franco supposed to get here?"

"You want me to show you, I'll show you," she said, swooping to the couch next to her tidy stack of health and senior magazines. "It's all here. Read it yourself for once." She began flipping the pages as if spanking them. She wanted him to see what she had seen in those pages, learn what she had learned, fear all that she feared. Lena had decided there would be no third stroke; after the last one Nick had stayed three weeks in Hartford Hospital, losing weight and color until his skin looked chalky as bread dough. She sat with him as long as the doctors would let her. She watched every pulse count, read every note on his chart. She challenged their choice of drugs and the amounts until they sent her away—sent her away!—as if she didn't know how to take care of her husband. They certainly didn't. Would they have bathed him if she hadn't complained? What young Dr. Kildare would have noticed that Nick fell asleep with a mouth full of oatmeal? He could have choked if she hadn't come to visit at that moment. No, no more strokes. You stay in the hospital too long, you get hurt. Or you die. Only God in heaven decided when that would happen, and He didn't need the help of doctors. She thumbed to an article—"Stopping Strokes at the Supper Table"—and reared to show him, but he shuffled past.

"Where are you going?"

"Blizzard's coming. I'm checking the furnace."

"That's silly, honey, the oil man was just here last month."

He walked past. He did not remember the visit of any oil man. Even if one had come, oil men could make mistakes that Lena couldn't catch. To her the furnace worked or it didn't.

At the cellar steps he balanced by holding the rail, each move made as if on ice. She held her breath, watching where he placed his slippered feet among the years of bundled newspapers, empty coffee cans, and paper grocery bags that crowded each narrow step. Something inside her clutched as if to keep him from falling. Going down was always the worst part. Even when he was young she had worried. "They're tricky, these steps," he used to say before dancing down them, showing off his agile footwork, then returning with a can of tomato sauce when she had asked for tuna, or sliced pineapple instead of pears, because (he would say) he had been dreaming of the delicate spray of freckles on her shoulders. Down he'd go again with a wink and a promise. Always gallant, that man, but so easily distracted by her even when she wasn't trying. And when she was trying, well— but so much had changed since his hands last touched her with the weightlessness of summer. Her back had bent, her knuckles gnarled like peach pits. His hands trembled now. His heart needed rest, not romance.

The cellar smelled of fusty cardboard. Drafts blew cold through the windows, which, at ground level outside, already cradled drifts of snow. Nick squinted through his bifocals at the oil gauge. He wet his thumb with the tip of his tongue and rubbed the glass, then leaned close. Rising on her toes behind him, Lena peered over his shoulder.

"We're safe," he said.

He folded his bifocals and tucked them in the pocket of his cardigan, then turned for a long, surprised look around the cellar: at his speed bag, so dry the leather had split like a lip; at a framed map of Italy, hung crooked, with the glass cracked from Bergamo to Genoa; at boxes of Christmas decorations hidden behind his workbench, untouched since he and Lena started spending the holiday with Franco and his family in balmy Atlanta, or Denise and hers in California. All of it, everything, made junk by time, dulled by a fuzz of dust.

"Jeez," he said. "Guess I've shirked my duties down here."

He pulled a handkerchief from his pants pocket, his brow already sweating at the thought of cleaning, organizing, discarding. Lena patted his back.

"Leave this be," she whispered.

★   ★   ★

"Well, if it isn't the lovely Mrs. Gionfriddo," Nick announced. With a sweep of his arm, he welcomed Ava to the house. She stumbled in, shimmying like a squirrel to shake snow from her green wool overcoat and her thin, impossible hair.

"C'mon in, honey," Lena said from the kitchen. "I didn't expect you today with the weather."

"Miss Nick's birthday? Nothing doing," Ava said. "But it wasn't easy. What is it? Twenty yards from my door to yours? It felt like it took ten years to get here."

"If it took ten years," Nick said, "that must make me eighty-four."

"Not a day over sixty, good-looking." Ava set aside a paper grocery bag in which she carried something, then worked the buttons of her coat. "Nick, would you?" she sang, lifting her arms and allowing him to help her. "Thank you," she said. "You're a prince. Happy birthday, sweetie."

Smiling, he pulled from the bag a pie still warm in its tin. Lena inhaled a deep breath of patience. "Sit," she said. "Everything's ready."

"Radio says we're in for it," Ava said. "More than twenty inches."

Lena ladled soup from a pot on the stove. "Did you stock up?"

"A volunteer from the senior center brought me some things last night."

"Why didn't you go out yourself? You can still drive. You stop doing things for yourself, you'll forget how."

Ava rolled her eyes at Nick as if they shared a private joke. "You think I'll forget how to grocery-shop?" she said to Lena. "I could be dead a dozen years, and if Stop & Shop had a special on Neapolitan ice cream I'd find it."

Lena served Ava first, then set before Nick a half bowl of steaming minestrone and a small plate of low-fat lasagna reheated from the night before.

"That's all?" he asked. "I'm pretty hungry."

"What I gave you is good."

"Lena," Ava said, "you know what they say. The way to a man's heart . . ." She reached over the margarine container and saccharin dish to pat Nick's belly.

"Any more stomach," Lena said, "and I'll lose the heart."

"A larger helping won't kill me. It's not like chocolate candy."

Lena glared as she sat down to her lunch. "Say grace," she ordered.

Nick led them through the blessing. That done, they talked of how the potholes would be wider once the snow melted and of how they worried about losing power, and they remembered shoveling out from the storms in '54 and '78 ("Backbreakers," said Nick). Ava sipped from her teacup and left lipstick prints on the edge. Lena had told her years before to blot, but Ava refused, and now lipstick leaked into the age lines above her lip. Lena kept silent and tried not to look at Ava's lips or the teacup. Nor did she speak when she noticed the snugness of Ava's dress. Ava had put on her winter pounds, the ones that had returned every year for the last thirty only to fade away in time for swimsuits. Ava was a miracle in that and so many other ways, the belle of the ball among men at the senior center.

Toward the end of lunch the telephone rang, and Nick pushed away from the table to answer. Lena shouted after him, "Is it Franco?"

"It's Denise," he yelled, "wishing me a happy birthday."

A few moments later he returned, thumbing toward the other room. "She wants to talk with you," he said without looking at his wife. "I don't know. Something about . . . I'm not sure what."

After Lena left for the phone, Ava edged her chair nearer to Nick, so near he noticed her purple eye shadow, his favorite color, and it reminded him of past purples: the silk tie from his sister on his twentieth birthday, the bicycle he'd found at the dump and rebuilt so Franco could ride with friends to school, the bruises over his ribcage from Tommy Duncan. "You want some apple pie?" Ava asked. He nodded, leaning nearer, and she cut him a slice. He forked a chunk, admiring it as if it were caviar. After he finished she said, "Nick, I've got to get back. I'd wait for Lena but I'm expecting a call myself, and I wonder would you walk me home? I worry about slipping."

He helped her into her coat, then retrieved his own from the hall closet. His galoshes he had left by the door after grocery shopping, and he felt pleased to remember. Fully bundled, he and Ava stepped outside into the wind and snow. Ava took Nick's arm, and his spine snapped straight. He flexed his biceps and his triceps, hoping that even through his heavy coat she would notice. "Don't let me fall," she shouted, and the two started next door, trudging through drifts, shoulders hunched and heads lowered against the gusts. At Ava's door she pecked him on the cheek good-bye.

Lena loved her daughter as much any mother has ever loved a child, but Denise talked too much. And now, having heard the kitchen door open and shut, Lena searched for a moment to interrupt Denise, sent love, and said good-bye. She found the deadbolt unlocked and Nick's galoshes missing. Through the window she saw snow ruffled in a wide path leading toward Ava's. Lena snatched her shawl from a peg near the door and stepped outside to the back stoop. Snowflakes pelted her face and dissolved in her eyes, their wetness like tears distorting her sight so that she couldn't be sure it was Nick walking toward her until she recognized his overcoat.

She bristled—a colicky child would be easier to nurse—but then he paused to look at something across the street, and she noticed how upright he seemed, how high he carried his head. He looked familiar, but in an out-of-context way, much like the time she met their parish priest, out of collar, at a city pool. With her shirt cuff she wiped snow from her eyes, but he remained unchanged from the moment before—still her husband but not her husband. And then she placed him: She had thought this Nick lived only in photo albums, in Christmases and birthdays past, lifting little Franco on his shoulders or playing third base at the company picnic. This Nick she had thought lost after his first stroke, but here he was, beautiful again and vital, and she felt a great reward for all her work. This, then, was the reason she gave so much, sacrificed her days to his care: this twinkling of health that brought his old self back to her, strokes be damned.

For a moment she lingered, admiring him as he faced across the street. Then, as she had when he was younger (working on the lawn or the car, and it was time to eat), she called his name. He turned toward her, saw her on the steps, but before she could wave his back curved, his shoulders slumped. He grimaced and looked at the place where snow collected around his feet. Her beautiful husband vanished quick as death.

She stopped breathing, then panicked, overwhelmed by a fear biting and sudden as a hot iron, and whose fault was that? The need to scold him knocked her like a spasm.

"Nick!" she shouted over the wind. "Nick! Come inside!"

And in that moment when she saw him as a child, when she wanted only to spank him and confine him to the safety of his recliner, she saw herself through his eyes—as a bitter medicine, punishing him with care. He shuffled inside, and when she touched him he stopped in complete obedience, clumps of snow sliding off his shoulders, turned to her and let her unbutton his wet, cold coat.

She led him to his recliner and wrapped him in a quilt she had sewn the winter before. His breath came in impatient snorts as if he awaited some chastisement.

"What were you doing out there, honey?" She tried to sound interested and casual.

"Ava worried about walking home, so I went with her."

"Ava could have waited for me," Lena said, then regretted it.

He said, "She thought I could handle it."

Lena tucked the quilt tighter, her fingers jabbing, cocooning him. "Well then, you did the right thing, didn't you? Ava's lonely. She needs the attention."

"Ava's all right." He rested his head against the pillow of the recliner, watched her face a moment and realized there would be no yelling. He relaxed, let a pleasant tiredness settle his breathing, push his eyelids closed. "Those Putnam boys," he mumbled. "Did you see them across the street? Building snowmen already. Can't be that fierce a blizzard if kids can play in it."

She said, "Maybe you should nap."

He nodded, eyes still shut, and she could count white bristles where he'd missed shaving along his jaw. She wanted suddenly to shave him. She had not shaved a man since her father when he could no longer hold a straight edge. His death had lasted a year and three months. A year and three months of profanity-laced rants against Roosevelt, the communists, and even against his daughter, who did not scrape his beard close enough to the skin. When he died she cried first with grief, then with joy, then with shame at her joy.

With a finger she stroked Nick's jawline and, noticing Ava's lipstick smear, wiped it away with her thumb, then cleaned the thumb on her apron. On her way to the kitchen she stopped at the living room window. The Putnam boys still rolled snow boulders around their yard. Already they'd created a family of snowmen.

"Nick?" she called, because she remembered a time the two of them had built snowmen together, and dressed them, and then in a giddy romp knocked them over with fists and shoulders and snow shovels. At the sound of her voice he opened his eyes a moment, then closed them. He drifted toward his own sleepy memory: of his sister the day before she died—in a fire so many decades past that no one talked about it anymore. They had met that day on Main Street outside Sage Allen's department store, an accident of chance that inspired her to throw her arms around him and laugh in his ear, leaving her lipstick on his lobe. She wiped it away between her forefinger and her thumb; the next day she vanished in a fire. In the world, then out.

★ ★ ★

WHRT announced a weather bulletin, and Lena stopped adding sugar to the ricotta to listen. Fourteen inches of snow, the man said, with at least ten more record-breaking inches expected. Bradley International Airport is closed, he added, nothing allowed in or out, as are all government offices except fire and police.

Franco won't make it, she thought. She poured the rest of the sugar and whipped the ricotta with her electric mixer until it swirled like cream. He would miss her cannoli. A special batch, too, made with a little extra cinnamon. More, then, for his father. Yes. She repeated it to herself. More for Nick on his birthday. Anything Ava could do for Nick, Lena had decided, she could do better. Flirt? Feed? Yes. If such things could return to her the husband she had married, then by God, more for Nick! She pulled the silver flatware from its place on a high shelf, dusted the box, and listened as those dessert forks rang against each other in a musical way, a sound she hadn't heard in her kitchen for so long, a song to herald Nick's resurrection, and with it her own. As she stuffed the shells, a glimpse of his pill container on the kitchen table gave her doubts. She repeated quietly to herself, "The only thing we have to fear. . . the only thing we have to fear . . ." and remembered how he had looked standing in the snow.

"Oh, hey . . . honey," he said later, ricotta stuck to a corner of his mouth. "This is ambrosia."

He watched her as he chewed the shells, as his tongue spread the ricotta around his mouth. She blinked, and he asked if she had a dust speck. "Eat," she said, then closed her eyes as if shutting something back. He took a second cannoli onto his plate. It was his birthday, but he ate fast before she changed her mind.

"Happy birthday, dear Nick," she sang, her voice almost a whisper, and she kissed his forehead. The phone interrupted. That would be Franco, she thought. Nick hurried to answer.

"Franco! We've been waiting to hear from you, kid." Nick leaned on the high back of the desk chair, too eager to sit. "Your plane get in okay?" He nodded into the phone, focusing on the desktop where they kept snapshots of Franco, Denise, the grandchildren, and the daily calendar with doctor appointments penciled in Lena's tight-looped cursive.

"LaGuardia's not that far. Why don't you rent a car and drive up? The fight's not until late. It's in Vegas, right? They're not snowed in there."

With the toe of his left slipper he bumped the desk leg and bumped it again. He shrugged, listened, bumped a few more times.

"So rent a four-wheel drive. C'mon, Franco. You've lived in Georgia too long. Kids are outside playing. The plows will clear the roads." He waved his free hand, chopping at the air, attacking it. Then he raised his arm over his head, palm forward, as if asking for quiet. "Yeah, yeah, you're right. That'd be crazy. So it's back to Atlanta, then? No, no. Sure. Yeah. There'll be other fights. You bet, Frankie. Sorry you couldn't make it. We'll see you another time."

He hung up, finger pressing the hook switch. With his other hand he lifted the receiver like a club, then thought better of it and rested it in its cradle. Nick started toward his chair, then stopped, moved another direction, slowly, randomly, like a used candy wrapper tossed by wind. He mouthed angry words as he clenched and unclenched his big fists.

Lena took up her mending. Since the first stroke this frightened her most, his confusion coupled with anger. She knotted the thread and bit it clean.

"Sit down," she said. "You're making me nervous."

He pitched himself into his recliner, then picked at threads in its upholstered arms, pulling them tight until they snapped.

★   ★   ★

"Big fight," said the grinning sportscaster on the six o'clock news. Yeah, yeah, thought Nick. "Snow will keep falling," said the frowning weatherman, "though winds have died. Watch for that freezing rain around midnight." Nick switched off the television, then stood at the front window. Outside looked as threatening as a Christmas card. The snow, floating toward lawns, roads, bushes, mailboxes, settled knee-deep. The lights of Preston Street reflected off the clouds and the snow so everything looked purple, even the smoke drifting from chimneys. Nobody stirred; only the Putnam boys' snow family dared the weather, and no vehicles drove the roads. How could Franco worry so much over an accident when no car was out there to hit? Hang that Franco, he thought. I'll drive myself.

He sneaked into the hall closet, wrestling on boots, overcoat, cap, and gloves; then, already winded, rushed out the door where jarring, silent cold enveloped him. Snow melted on his cheeks as he stood in the quiet, admiring the bruised face of the moon that peeked through a clearing in the clouds, and the great frozen spread that had shut down all of Hartford. A city truck plowed past, scraping asphalt and wrecking the snow. From the driveway he watched it, then looked around wondering what it was had brought him out into the cold. Not to shovel. Not to toboggan. Across the street in the Putnams' yard, he saw, were four snowmen, and he remembered Tommy Duncan, and he shook out his arms. Hitting something, he thought. That would feel good. Maybe that's why I came out here.

He crossed his yard, then climbed the bank the plow had pushed against the roadside, snow sticking to his boots in such hefty clumps that even this short walk fatigued him. Panting, he climbed the opposite snowbank and reached the Putnams' with his undershirt dampened by sweat, chilling him to shivers. The snowmen had no eyes that he could see, their hats were crowned with white, and each carrot nose bore an inch of the stuff along its length. He flicked one with his finger. The carrot popped out and landed, sank, vanished.

"You think I'm old, don't ya?" he said. "I got enough for you, Frosty."

Frosty held his ground.

"Some kinda tough bastard, huh?"

Nick cocked his left shoulder, pulled back for the big roundhouse, the punch he almost never used, but he wanted it now, wanted to throw everything he had, empty it all so he'd feel spent and not just weary, leave himself scattered like Frosty's head across the Putnams' front yard. He connected, but there was no explosion of white. The head was heavy with wet—it felt like he'd punched a concrete slab— and the head cracked in two, falling off the body.

Nick kept the pain tight, wouldn't shout even though his left hung loose in its glove like peanuts in a bag, even though his legs shuddered beneath him, his lungs couldn't find enough air, and his head reeled like a carnival ride.

But the roundhouse. The roundhouse had worked.

Yeah, if the target's a stiff.

He needed a corner. So he sat. Right there in the Putnams' front yard at the foot of the snowman he had decapitated. He sank into the pillow of snow, which welcomed him warm and cozy. From the sky it alighted around him, on him, sprinkling before his eyes like confetti, filling his head.

Nick was not in his chair. Don't go chasing, she told herself, not like last time. But two buttons later, he hadn't returned. "Nick?" she yelled, loud enough to carry through the house, in a tone to which he always responded. Only the radiator knocked in answer. A moment later she called down to the cellar. She started then to pray her "Please

God" prayer before hurrying to each room in a house suddenly too large. Nick was not dead in their bedroom, or in the pantry, or on the back porch. Then, passing the living room window, she saw him near the body of a snowman in the Putnams' front yard. She watched him struggle to stand and foresaw every consequence of his effort: a broken hip or concussion, or a clot pumped furiously toward a narrow vein.

She ran—no shawl, no coat—in house slippers that soaked up the cold and the wet so that her feet ached before she reached him. Her arms surrounded him, tried to crush him, and he felt so cold, so cold.

"Damn you," she said, crying through clenched jaws. "Damn you, Nick DiFiore."

"Lena," he said. "I got tired is all."

She heard a door open, then shouting—the Putnams—and she knew that in moments they'd surround her and Nick, and they would see how she had failed him, how nearly she had lost him. No, she would protest, arms clamped around his body, her bone-cold fingers seeking him beneath the layers of coat, sweater, shirt, needing again to hold too tightly. You're wrong, she would say. You're wrong. I love him better than this.

The Greatest Show

No circus today.

That's what we wrote on sheets of scratch paper. We used square-tipped marking pens that squeaked on the slick poster board and gave off fumes. We wrote in red and purple and blue. We knew the circus couldn't happen. Not that day.

Violetta was twelve then, a pixie in star-embroidered bell-bottoms and threadbare ballet slippers, pit-patting on concrete floors, through tunnels and concourses and the exhibition hall, whispering at every-body to hurry. We'd only begun to set up for that night's show, the first of a three-day stand. Ring carpets needed mopping, and the trapeze was a half-erected tangle of cables and pulleys and ropes. But we stopped everything to gather around television sets—in the dressing room, in Fritz's trailer office—and watch. We covered our mouths with our hands or pressed fists against our eyes, just as people did everywhere, and in the dressing room Schmautz demanded we turn it off, but we didn't turn it off.

No circus today. Postponed. New Dates and Times TBA.

On with the show means something to us, it really does, but times come when what matters doesn't. Carrying our signs and tape, we crisscrossed the downtown of that week's stop—Hartford, the capital of Connecticut—and we posted the announcements that our show would not go on. The pointless paperwork of bystanders.

★ ★ ★

In the arena, the bears ate dried fruit, and the lions tore at deer carcasses—roadkill Marcus had bought from New York's highway department. Fritz watched the news in his trailer office. Fritz is our ringmaster. It's difficult to guess his age because he shaves his head twice each day. Fritz carries such girth that he leans back when he walks; his chest holds lungs you'd swear could inflate truck tires. Fritz wrestled in college until he broke a man's back. They had been opponents since high school and competed with the fierceness of brothers. The man lived, but neither he nor Fritz ever wrestled again. Fritz flunked out of school because it was the easiest way to leave, and he picked up as a roustabout with a show that came through Iowa City.

That afternoon, after we finished posting signs, Fritz wandered alone through Hartford's downtown. On an overpass, he leaned into the chain-link meant to keep suicides off the interstate below, and he bird's-eyed the traffic, loud and hot. He looked hard to see people, it mattered to him that he see people and not just cars, and he picked up flashes of a woman's long hair, of an elbow propped where the driver's window had been lowered, of a hand that tossed a cigarette butt. He imagined a heart attack, onset of diabetic coma, a lunge for a ringing cell phone dropped too near the brake pedal, and he pictured cars spinning into each other and past each other, steel tearing, horns wailing, asphalt gouged, a work boot detached from a body lying on its side near a painted white line. He saw this so clearly that he was surprised, now, to notice traffic traveling unimpeded. He let go of the fence links, and his skin had creased where he'd gripped too hard.

In front of a closed and caged store stocked with athletic shoes and imitation Rolex watches, he met a fellow with a West Indian lilt who sold electronics from the back of a white and rusted van. Fritz dickered because Fritz always dickers. The electronics salesman smoothed his Old Testament beard and said, "None of this haggling, mister. Not today. It's not right. Take the price or leave it," and Fritz felt a prick of shame that turned his ears hot and, he felt certain, red. He decided to buy two portable TVs instead of just one, as if twice the purchase could atone for his mistake. But walking away with two TVs he didn't need, he just felt stupid. In his trailer office he moved aside his checkerboard and his portable whiskey bar to make room for the extra sets. A couple of roustabouts helped him rewire the satellite connections, and he was pleased to find his new TVs worked. He watched his old set and his two new ones at the same time, a different news network on each. The electronics salesman, he decided, was a cynic but clever in how he got his asking price. What people won't do on the worst days. He dialed his mother's number in Des Moines, but her line was busy.

Most of us stayed that afternoon in the bowels of the arena. We lay on cots or watched updates on the news. We'd hired the day laborers, so they still worked, draping black plastic sheets over the walls and floors where we planned to keep the animals. Blackness filled that wide hallway, blanketed the walls as high as the ceilings, and the blackness shifted as people walked on it, whispered with each footfall, reflected pinpricks of fluorescent light as if the midnight sky had collapsed and settled in that spot. "Today, like mourning cloth," said Hezekiah as he swept piss-soaked wood shavings out of his bear cages and onto the black plastic, then spread fresh bedding. We all paid more attention to the animals, especially the ponies, scratching their ears, gazing into the bottomless liquid of their eyes. A lion's roar echoed through the tunnels, redundant and hollow, something we'd usually ignore but sounding that day like a desperate, repeated shout of the same word, a word that came close to explaining how we all felt, but then the lion grew tired and huffed a while, then quieted.

Violetta gravitated from television set to television set, staring at the screens, in tears. Her mother pulled her away and pulled her away again, but Violetta always returned. Violetta's romance with suffering and disaster was probably normal in a girl her age, but it troubled her mother, who had no other child and had always lived for her daughter's happiness. When Violetta was an infant and resisted breast-feeding, Ursula paid a man to tattoo Violetta's name and a thornless red rose onto Ursula's right breast. The pain from the needles shot through to her knees and toes and crotch, but all suffering went away when her daughter started to nurse.

So on this day, Ursula kissed Violetta's pale forehead, took her hand, and led the girl out of the arena's gloom. Ursula recalled a stop in Hartford a few years earlier when she and Violetta had enjoyed a carousel ride in a downtown park. She remembered the horses as grotesque and beautiful, aberrations of action, their lips and teeth gargantuan, manes lacquered and glossy, each horse ornamented with reins and saddles of silver and cherry. She remembered Violetta talking of the horses for days.

The park's grass was September worn. Though a sign announced open hours on Tuesdays, mother and daughter found the carousel shut inside its pavilion, dark and without music. Ursula pressed her face to the glass to see the motionless shadows inside. When finally she turned away from the pavilion and her own disappointment, she saw her daughter crouched nearby at the edge of a tiny park pond. The water's surface sat stagnant, coated with pollen and pigeon down, dotted with soda cups. "I can ride real ponies anytime I want," Violetta said. She fingered bottle caps and paper clips and the broken tines of plastic forks, and she tossed them one by one into the water, the pollen so thick the surface showed no ripples. Violetta waited to see whether each thing she'd thrown would sink or float, then she tossed something else. She told her mother she wanted everything to sink. After a while her mother wanted that, too.

★ ★ ★

No one ever figured out how Ted and Rosa got into the building, which was supposed to be locked. Schmautz the Clown met them in a concourse. He told us later that he'd been practicing his greeting routine, the one he uses to welcome kids as they scramble into the exhibition hall. He'd put on his polka-dot costume, but not his makeup or cone-head cap, and he pantomimed greetings to pretend children, waving his monkey puppet. He told us that a man and a woman walked down the tunnel toward him.

"No circus today, folks," he told them.

The man nodded toward the monkey dangling from Schmautz's hand. "How about a smidgen more of that puppet?" he said. "What we saw looked pretty good."

What's Schmautz going to do? He worked the monkey so it blew kisses to the strangers. "Say hello to Betty," said Schmautz.

"Hello, Betty," said the man. The puppet shook hands with the strangers. The woman stood an inch taller than the man in her black sandals with slight heel, and she looked younger, even discounting hair coloring. Trim, she was dressed in black linen slacks and a white sleeveless blouse, collar upturned, hair spiked as if she meant to intimidate other country-club wives but not alienate them. He wore clean white sneakers, pressed slacks and work shirt, sleeve cuffs buttoned at the wrist, very un-circus. Dime-store eyeglasses poked from his breast pocket, and the skin at his throat pimpled as if he had shaved with a played-out razor. The man and woman looked like each other in that way married couples do because time and happenstance have beaten and fed and comforted them in similar ways.

The man studied Schmautz's face, but if he was looking for something in particular he didn't say, and Schmautz felt unfinished and wished he had put on makeup after all. The woman said, "We had planned to come today. We're from out of town." She spoke with one of those honeysuckle drawls that makes you crave red velvet cake if you've ever been south.

The man said, "I was born here, in Hartford," which showed he understood us. Sometimes we forget where we are.

They explained that they'd bought tickets online. They'd come from North Carolina. Not just for the circus, no. "Well, yes," he admitted. "Crazy as that might sound." She corrected him. "Whimsical," she said. "Not crazy."

But then they had found themselves alone that morning in a hotel room watching it all on television, and they hated that, hated the packets of coffee and the inoffensive wallpaper and the fifth-floor windows that didn't open. The man said, "We couldn't sit in the room all day. We can't fly home. We didn't know what else to do." He handed their tickets to Schmautz.

Schmautz didn't know what to do, either. The show had been scheduled for eight, and it was hours earlier than that. Besides, there was no show. He gave the tickets back, but waved the couple toward the exhibition hall. "We never finished setting up," he told them. He smoothed the nylon fur of Betty's head. "Might be a juggler or a hula-hoop dancer running through a routine. Ask Hezekiah to show you a bear."

The woman started toward the exhibition hall, but the man lingered, and Schmautz again wished he'd worn makeup. He raised the monkey puppet in front of his face, had Betty wave good-bye to the man, who reached out to scratch under Betty's chin. Then the man laid a hand on Schmautz's padded shoulder. "Must be hot in that outfit," he said. Said Schmautz: "You know it, brother." The woman reached back for her husband's hand, and they slow-stepped down the tunnel, the squeak of his sneakers repeating off the bright walls. Schmautz kept on with his Betty routine, greeting kids who weren't there.

★ ★ ★

In the arena, roustabouts wiped dirt from the ring curves and stuck light poles into tripods. Chico, the crew chief, had decided to work himself and his crew extra hard, as if the president himself had deemed a fully assembled circus as necessary to national morale. Z, a Yaqui from Mexico who was our newest hire, couldn't get the lights right, and Chico yelled at him, "Damn, Z! This ain't no reservation. It's a plantation, motherfucker. Get the work done or I'll trade you in, get me another." Z said nothing, just plugged together a different combination of cords and when the bulbs lit moved on to another set.

Our roustabouts come from everywhere, and they are cruel to each other, and they defend each other like family, and some nights would cut each other's throats. They know better than any of us that a circus is a heavy thing. They push lions' steel cages into the arenas and push them out. They unroll the ring carpets, then roll them up again and heave them onto carts. In non-union towns, which is most everywhere, they drive forklifts to haul equipment canisters from our trucks into the arenas and back again. They carry the shovels and the pulleys and cable spools, and they lift and assemble the platforms that allow four-year-olds to climb onto the backs of elephants at five dollars a ride. When the show starts, crowds see tapestries and light, airy trapezes, an ephemerality that arrives and vanishes with a clap of thunder or burst of smoke. If people understood the full weight of the show they watch, they would be crushed. The roustabouts bear it piece by muscle-tearing piece. They raise it in a day. They dismantle it in a few hours, leaving no sign that it ever was.

It's hard to say how long the man and woman sat that afternoon watching Chico's people work. Eventually they stepped out of the stands and approached Z.

"We apologize for the intrusion . . . ," said the man.

"Will anyone perform?" asked the woman. "The clown said someone might."

Z rose off his knees. He tucked a screwdriver into his baggy bluejeans pocket, then straightened his dark sweatshirt with a tug. Arenas are cold even in summer. The woman had goosebumps on her tanned arms. Z nodded politely.

"Hey, people," called Chico, who had stepped near. "Y'all have to go. We're shut down."

"A juggler or something," said the woman as if she were championing the last wish of a dying child. "The clown said—"

"I don't care about the clown," Chico said. "Today's too real, is all. Circus ain't right."

"We bought tickets," said the woman.

Chico wiggled his tongue through the gap where he had no front teeth. He did not need the last word. He trusted Fritz to do the right thing.

★ ★ ★

Fritz had been sitting in his trailer office in the dark, miniblinds drawn to cut screen glare as he watched the news on three TVs and sipped whiskey. Now he tugged a string and let bright sun in on the couch where the man and woman sat. Daylight washed colors out of the pictures on the TVs. Fritz offered his bottle, then poured the shots. He felt glad for the company. The woman said their names: Ted and Rosa Liszak of Raleigh, North Carolina. She practiced law. He had just sold a regional magazine business and was starting an early retirement. As the three talked, Ted worried a red checker piece between his forefinger and thumb.

"Didn't you see the signs?" asked Fritz.

"They broke our hearts," answered Ted, and he smiled. "We hurried in case you were leaving town."

"There's really nothing for you here," said Fritz.

"You don't know us that well," said Rosa.

"I know what's appropriate given what happened this morning."

Rosa's glare dared Fritz to insult her again. "We're not cruel or stupid," she said. "We could have watched TV in our hotel room and drunk our own whiskey."

Fritz swirled the ice in his glass and grinned. He liked that this woman could say something harsh and make it sound like a compliment. Maybe it was a southern thing. Or a lawyer thing. Meanwhile, her husband studied old photos on the trailer's walls—of Fritz as a roustabout, then as a performer juggling fiery torches. Ted studied it a while, said, "I've always wondered what kind of person joins the circus."

"Some are born into it," Fritz said. "Mostly, everybody's got a different reason."

On one of the networks the hour scheduled for the president's first public address crawled across the screen. Another network showed a map of where everything had happened. Fritz said, "Folks, I'm sorry if I insulted you. I'm just surprised you're here."

Ted flipped the checker piece as if it were a coin, heads or tails. "I haven't been to a show since I was a toddler," he said. "But you could almost say I was born into the circus." He unbuttoned the cuff of his right sleeve and pushed it back to show skin embossed over every inch with scars. Some scars were lavender and others gray and some were pigmentless as teeth.

Fritz called a meeting: performers, roustabouts, everybody. We gathered near the animal cages, the black plastic sheeting rustling beneath our feet, the bears pacing on their leashes and a lion licking the mesh of its cage. Ursula sat on a straw bale, her daughter in her lap. Schmautz had tied a knot in Betty's arms and hung her around his neck. She lay against his back, head lolling to the left, glass eyes sightless.

Ted, Fritz told us, had last visited a circus in 1944.

We know circus history, and word of Ted's scars had spread fast, so we understood. His last circus had been a famous one, when the Ringling big top burned right there in Hartford. It's a tale every circus performer with a few years on the road has heard, a story that for us distinguishes Hartford from a Morgantown or a Schenectady or Terre Haute. It begins with a matinee and a tent waterproofed with paraffin. Wartime. July's worst heat. Hundreds of women and children panting and sticky in folding chairs in the bleachers. Then the tent catches fire.

No one knows why. A lot of people die. Some sixty years later, we still try for a better performance in Hartford. We don't take the blame for history. We're not Ringling. We're a chicken-dinner outfit from Branson hired for county fairs and Shriner shows. We feel no responsibility for a gas-soaked rag of a tent that collapsed on a crowd decades before most of us were born. But we're not heartless. So Hartford always gets a little extra.

"But not today, right?" said Chico, his tongue flicking through the gap in his teeth. "My people ain't done setting up. Give history a rain check."

"No rain checks," said Fritz. "I've been on the phone. Home office wants us to cancel the whole Hartford run. Pick up again in Rutland, maybe. For these two, it's today or not at all."

Renato, the father in our family of aerialists, said no, absolutely not, but Schmautz the Clown wanted to. Chico insisted his crew get its regular take for a full house. "This is charity," said Schmautz. Chico said, "Charity is when they bring the crippled kids. This is nuts." And Ursula suggested that if we did charity, we should do it where people were suffering right now.

That got everyone quiet. Then someone said, "People suffer everywhere all the time. It's all pain, right? How does a little clowning make anything worse?"

The argument lasted awhile. It was strange. Ted and Rosa hadn't asked for the whole circus; they hadn't asked for all three rings. But we chewed on each other as if this decision mattered more than any we'd ever made. Maybe we were asking each other for permission to go ahead or to refuse. In the end, Hezekiah said he'd bring out his bears, and Ursula agreed to let Violetta perform her hula-hoop dance. That would have been enough, but Schmautz said he'd go, too, and so did Mad Dog the Daredevil Cyclist and Nabeela the Stilt Walker.

Fritz offered the roustabouts half pay, and Chico said "not enough to blaspheme this day," but in the circus everyone works as an independent contractor, and in this circus everyone works for Fritz. Some roustabouts took the money. Mad Dog assembled his Death Sphere, and Hezekiah and Marcus erected the animal cage around the center ring. Roustabouts tested the sound system and lights, and others climbed into the stands to run the spots. Watching, you'd think the preparations were the usual. Ursula helped her daughter stretch while the girl listened to hip-hop on tiny headphones; Hezekiah brushed wood shavings from his bears' fur; Schmautz and the clowns painted their faces; Fritz pomaded his mustache. But that day, as the arena echoed with the clanging of cage doors and the now-and-then roar of a beast, we kept a religious silence. Whatever performance we were about to give would be governed by new rules. We dressed in our leotards and sequins, clown wigs and capes. Fritz visited us one by one. "Forget the day," he told us. "Or remember it. Whichever helps."

The house lights darkened. Spotlights blinded us as they always blind us. The speakers shuddered with our thunder-and-electronics fanfare, less Sousa than video-game theme. Out of habit, we expected applause. We listened for it. Who knows why Ted and Rosa didn't clap. But the absence of applause was the first flaw.

That late afternoon, each of us who stepped in the rings felt a new and desperate need to nail every handspring, to catch every juggled plate. No one spoke of this, but we saw it in each other, the ways we attacked our performances. That morning the world had been reborn— in grief and violence, yes—but we knew we stood at the beginning of something. Whatever that new thing was to become, we wanted to get our part right. We wanted to be as good as the Bolshoi or the Ziegfeld Follies, and somehow trusted we could. But Nabeela tumbled from his stilts. Marcus couldn't get the lions to do anything but run circles around the caged ring. Roustabouts dialed up the wrong music, playing the aerialists' melody during the clowns' bank-robbery skit and the bank-robbery tune during Mad Dog's dirt-bike ride inside the Sphere of Death. We were jinxed. Miriam the Acrobatic Scarf Dancer became tangled in her knots. Schmautz, who was to enter the ring after her, slipped away and closed himself in the men's room. It sounded vicious, his kicking the doors of the stalls and shouting, kicking and shouting, the doors crashing against their frames. At that moment, Fritz was calling into the P.A., announcing Hezekiah and his bears.

From the deepest backwoods and piney hollows of Arkansas, The Ozark Mountain Bear Devils!

Dressed in hillbilly garb, accompanied by Hezekiah in his coon-skin cap and fringed buckskin, Ma, Pa, and Daisy Mae Bear waddled into the ring. With the long stock of his whip, Hezekiah prodded the bears to walk on barrels and stand on their heads. When one bear performed, Hezekiah sent the other two to sit in rocking chairs where roustabouts kept them occupied with dog biscuits. Hillbilly saws and fiddles played over the speakers, and Hezekiah signaled thumbs up to the roustabout running the soundboard.

The bears cavorted along a balance beam, Pa and Ma dismounting through a hoop at one end. Then Hezekiah twisted open the propane tank under the hoop and with a wand-lighter ignited the hoop's gas jets into a halo of flame. Now, the recorded drum roll. Black smoke roiled; fire snapped. Daisy Mae Bear hesitated. Hezekiah jerked his head toward the hoop. Fritz pleaded, *Let's give Daisy Mae some encouragement, ladies and gentlemen!* But Ted and Rosa said nothing. The fire made shadows that fluttered across their bodies. We hadn't thought things through. Ted crouched forward, head bowed, resting his elbows on his knees. Rosa leaned into her husband, one hand stroking the length of his back. But Hezekiah didn't see this. He concentrated on his bear. He wanted to get things right. Daisy Mae barked her fear. Hezekiah poked with his whip stock at Daisy Mae's hind legs, then gave her a bite from the lash. Daisy Mae—morose, chagrined— leaped sideways off the beam, away from the fiery hoop, but bumped it with her rump so the hoop teetered and fell. The hoop kept burning, and roustabouts ran into the ring to save the carpet. Those who stood near could smell the bear's singed, acrid fur.

Intermission! Fritz growled into his microphone.

★ ★ ★

We watched Ted walk his wife to the ladies' room, steering her with an arm around her shoulders. We left him alone while he waited for her, let him roam places we wouldn't usually allow ticket holders. He fingered the spot where fire had fallen and the ring carpet melted.

Ursula did not want to watch him, as some of us were doing. Her insides felt awful, as though stuffed with something gritty and poisonous, and watching Ted she felt sicker. She followed Rosa into the ladies' room where Rosa stood before a mirror, and Ursula thought she might be crying. When Rosa finally spoke, what she said sounded like an accusation.

She said, "There's no comfort in this."

"It's not much of a show," said Ursula. She stepped near and dipped her hands into a sink basin. Its automatic faucet ran cold water. "Is he all right?"

"Pulse racing. Skin clammy. Soul sick. The fire took us by surprise."

"We use lots of fire. It's in the juggling act, the motorcycle act . . . "

Rosa waved an end to the list. "He's never had problems as long as I've known him. Campfires. Gas-burning stoves. Bonfires on the beach. It was his birthday last week. Sixty candles all aflame. No trouble."

"This is different."

"Apparently." Rosa dabbed a tissue against a faucet's mouth, then wiped around the rims of her red eyes; she had been crying. "He's always loved this city—for no reason I understand. 'It's my birthday,' he said. 'What the heck,' he said, like he was invulnerable. 'Let's go to the circus.'"

"Then today happened," Ursula said. She blinked to check her own tears.

"He wanted to see the aerialists. 'I can do without the animal tricks,' he said. 'I want to see the man on the flying trapeze.' Does that sound strange? I'm sorry I snapped at you. It's the mother in me. I want to beat up the bully and hug the child."

"We're not bullies."

"The circus hurt him. That confuses the issue."

"My name's Ursula," said Ursula. She reached for Rosa's hands, which felt cool. "My daughter is Violetta. She's the hula-hoop dancer."

Rosa paused as if deciding something. "It's my pleasure to meet you," she said.

"You have kids?" Ursula asked.

"In North Carolina. They're scared. We talked by telephone. That's all."

"I wish they had come with you. It's not much of a circus without children."

"Ours are too old for the circus, and not yet old enough."

When the women emerged, Ted met them and touched Rosa's hand, the touch brief, as if sufficient to confirm what years of marriage gave them to understand. Then Ursula asked Violetta to show Ted and Rosa around, to name for them each lion and chimpanzee, to show how Mad Dog's two-stroke motocross cycle stayed on the high wire and how so many clowns could fit into such a picayune car. "If we can't give you a good show," said Ursula, "at least we can pull the curtain back."

Violetta wore a blue terry-cloth bathrobe over her outfit, and fishnet stockings and high heels that clicked on the concrete. At the lion cages, she warned Ted and Rosa to stand a good three feet away. "That's what we tell everyone," she said. She used her hands to emphasize each word. "*A good three feet.* But I've petted the lions before. I sneak up when they aren't looking." Then she asked, "Can I see your burns?"

Ted turned to face the girl. "Aren't you brave," he said.

"Show her, honey," said Rosa.

He unbuttoned his sleeves and pushed them high as if preparing for a blood pressure exam. Then he stretched his exposed arms forward. He extended his palms and his fingers, and he turned his wrists over and back so Violetta could see the skin's stitchings. "This is only some," he said. "I have scars all on my legs and chest and belly and back." Violetta walked nearer. Ted nodded, and she traced lines on his arms with a small finger.

"They're not so bad anymore," Ted told her. "It's hard to tell old man skin from old scars. When I was your age, that's when I looked like a lizard."

"They're pretty," said Violetta.

"Lifelong friends." He waved an arm once more as he finished buttoning.

"The fire scared you, didn't it?"

"I suppose it did. I was a boy. I can't remember."

"The fire scared you today."

"Oh. Not so much. I knew I was safe. Apparently my body remembers what I can't."

The three came to the room we'd turned into a mess hall, where Chico had plugged in his electric coffeepot and where he kept a bottle of jalapeño-salted peanuts no one else could touch. We had a box of cold-cut subs, too, sandwiches we'd picked up frozen from a caterer in Albany. A few of us were eating and talking: about the day, and about Ted, and about how everything had gone so awry. We stopped when our guests arrived. Fritz invited them to sit, asked if they'd like a soggy sandwich. We made the smallest of small talk amidst long silences, and now and then someone would leave the room and come back with a report from the TV.

A moment came when we all were quiet, and Ted cleared his throat. "I shouldn't have come today," he said. "It was selfish." The fluorescent bulbs above him flickered, brightening, then darkening, then brightening his tan face. Rosa whispered to him, but he shook his head, chasing away her suggestion.

Schmautz said, "We're not done. Give us a chance. We'll figure it out."

"It won't get better," said Chico. "You got no sense of decency. Y'all are dancing on graves."

"Shut up," said Schmautz. "Shut up. Shut. Up."

A roustabout put hands on Schmautz's shoulders to keep him in his seat. It was a kindness. Chico would have torn the old clown apart.

"I don't know what's decent," said Hezekiah.

"Nothing's decent," said Fritz. "Everything's decent."

The *fup-fup* of pigeon wings in the rafters startled us. Once we decided the pigeon didn't belong to the clowns, Chico chucked a wad of tinfoil its way. The pigeon chased the foil ball to the floor in a corner of the room and pecked at it.

Hezekiah asked Ted, "What was it like the day of the fire?"

Ted wiped his mouth with a paper napkin. "Not like today," he said. "The country didn't much notice. There was no cable TV. And there was a war going on."

"But lots of people died," someone protested.

"Almost a hundred and seventy. Not so many, when you consider."

"You can't make those comparisons," said Rosa.

"We compare every day," said Chico. "People die all the time, but it's some days that who dies or how or how many makes the whole country notice. Other days not. That's truth."

Ted said, "The fire mattered in Hartford—the deaths and the survivors, at least—for a few years. The nuns at school let me get away with more mischief than other kids. Now it's an old story, and who cares?"

Fritz folded his sandwich wrapper. "Intermission's over. We've got a performance to finish. No fire in the second act."

"We've caused enough trouble," said Ted.

"I want a show," said Fritz. "A show needs an audience."

Ted studied Fritz, and it seemed he was contemplating the consequences of crossing a man that large who had shared his whiskey. "We owe you that," Ted said. Then he and Rosa walked with Hezekiah back to the exhibition hall. The rest of us gathered our garbage, which smelled of salami and mustard, and tossed it into pails near the door. Fritz, apropos of nothing, said, "Bloody hell," and kicked a table leg so hard Chico's coffeemaker tumbled. Schmautz lifted Betty and looked into her face. He covered her glass eyes with his hand. Schmautz said,

"I once met a Chinese man on a bus who told me he lived through Tiananmen Square. He talked too much, and after a while I changed seats." He shook his head at himself. The pigeon had returned to the heights of air ducts and fluorescent lights, and it cooed. Schmautz dropped his garbage into the can, then swung Betty by the arms as he walked from the room. Violetta asked Fritz, "What's Tinmen Square?"

★ ★ ★

Ladies! Gentlemen! Boys and girls! Children of every age! Welcome back to a world of marvels and imagination, wrought by devils and angels, kings and fools!

Dancers and acrobats flashed through the center ring in bright-shining leotards, and for the first time Ted and Rosa acknowledged us. Elephants lifted into handstands, and our tiny audience clapped. A monkey played "Ode to Joy" on a squeaky violin, and Ted and Rosa cheered. Their praise echoed in the hall, and it sounded as if there were dozens of Teds and Rosas. They banged the metal legs of their folding chairs on the concrete floor. They stepped into the stands and stomped their feet. They clapped so hard their palms must have stung. We've known louder audiences and larger ones, too, but none more enthusiastic. They offered us honest appreciation, the sort that keeps us roaming from city to city. That applause changed us, and yes, we nailed our performances. Even that day when events had shoved in our faces that circus work was trivial and measly and low, Ted and Rosa's applause helped us embrace the optimism of our craft. One after another we stood clarified in the spotlight, feeling important once again and perhaps even necessary.

And now, Fritz's voice boomed over the loudspeakers, repeating what we'd heard—with slight variations—hundreds of times before . . .
Please watch carefully
(because Ted, this is for you!)
As we present
Our Grand Finale

Unbound by the physical laws of nature
Loosed from the cares of this Earth
the incomparable Cavalcade of Circus Stars!
Roustabouts whirled the spotlights helter-skelter across the hall, and the procession began—as it always does—with the elephants. Stepping slow. Following the oval track around the rings, their trunks swinging to and fro, their diadems flickering in the starry lights of the disco balls. And then the performers. Alice the Sword Swallower. Frankie the Escape Artist. Clowns with ruby-painted skin. Violetta with angel wings. Mist from dry ice wafted across the rings, changing colors as spotlights flashed red, purple, and blue, green and orange, as if the mist were thunderheads concealing popsicle-colored lightning. Sasha's yellow horse cantered forth with patriotic streamers tied to its tail and a rooster riding in its saddle. A clown with donkey ears played accordion. Even Renato's family, who had not performed on high, came tumbling across the floor, human pinwheels of color and light. From the loudspeakers played a piano waltz that might have issued from a tawdry French café, not our usual finale theme but no mistake, either, chosen by a roustabout who understood the day, who gave us a delicate and awkward tune, one sad and off-balance, teetering, uncertain, played as if it resisted playing but had no choice. Ted and Rosa waltzed in slow time with the music, and for a moment a roustabout caught their elegant ease in a spotlight. As the last performer marched into the hall, Fritz strolled behind him, his high collar buttoned and his stovepipe hat tall, and he became the end of the procession and its beginning. We started a second turn, then a third, a fourth, a slow-motion merry-go-round, cheering and waving toward the surrounding shadow.

Then Fritz led us into the rings. We made such an assembly of wonder. He took his microphone from his pants pocket, and he called out his traditional farewell . . .

That's the show, ladies and gentlemen, boys and girls. Thank you for coming. Please drive safely. Go now, and remember to make every day a circus day. Good-bye! Good-bye, and Godspeed! Good-bye!

We waved as if the exhibition hall were emptying soul by soul of grandparents and grandchildren, of young mothers, of toddlers and teens, of faces we loved and would miss. We waved to Ted and Rosa who waved back, smiling, standing. An ovation. We could have stayed in those rings forever.

But house lights came up, glaring and harsh. We blinked away our blindness, let the exhibition hall regain its shapes.

"Holy Lord Jesus," said Schmautz.

People in the stands stood, and some applauded, people who were scattered in all directions. We saw children and parents holding children. Thirty people, maybe, or forty. More were coming. They stepped from the concourses and searched the hall for seats, or they looked at us and pointed, whispering in children's ears. It was near eight o'clock, almost show time. A man wearing a Red Sox cap and carrying a toddler with pierced ears came near Hezekiah and asked if he needed tickets. Hezekiah shook his head, and the man nodded, turned back toward the seats and said into his cell phone, "Free show, man. I'm telling you. Hustle your ass down here."

So eight o'clock came, and a crowd filled the hall's lower level. We didn't argue. *Ladies!* shouted Fritz. *Gentlemen! Boys and girls!*

Schmautz mimed for children, and Mad Dog roared up the high wire. Fritz told the roustabouts not to charge for elephant rides at intermission, but yes for cotton candy. We still had no trapeze, and Hezekiah—thinking his bears had endured enough—kept them in their cages. We were distracted, yes. We felt the burden survivors feel, the juggling act of pity and grief and celebration for the good that's left. Violetta finished her hula-hoop dance, then she and Ursula embraced in the darkness at the edge of the rings and sobbed.

Now it's hundreds of shows later. Late nights, after Fritz and Hezekiah and Mad Dog are back from billiards, or when we take a break after we've set up for another show, we sometimes tell each other stories of that day. We shake our heads in disbelief and try to gather the parts we've lost, trying to remember—for example—which of us discovered the next morning that someone had torn down our postponement signs and crumpled them into trash cans around downtown Hartford. Chico has since quit our circus, and Schmautz retired to a trailer near Destin, and we've lost what they would have remembered (we can't always remember what we want to remember), so the stories change. Violetta insists she rode the park carousel that day, and Ursula says no. Fritz can't remember how much he paid for his TVs. Our sense of the day fades. We're left with a few facts, a recollection of dread and joy, and a sense that every damn thing disappears too quickly. Lucky us.

In the hubbub of that second show, we lost track of Ted and Rosa. That was okay. We figured they'd left the arena, just snuck away with the crowd. We cleaned elephant shit from inside the rings, laundered sweaty leotards, paused to watch on TV where news camera lights still shined on vivid faces.

But later, when Hezekiah went to the staging area to check on his bears, he found Ted and Rosa sitting near the cage, a step or two from where Daisy Mae slept, tranquilized and snoring, her singed haunches waffled against the bars. Hezekiah had come in quietly, not disturbing the black plastic sheets, and Ted and Rosa hadn't noticed him. They sat on wooden stools pushed close together, him on the right, her on the left. They leaned so their shoulders touched. They watched Daisy Mae breathe, and they talked, but what they said Hezekiah couldn't hear. They held hands. With his free hand, Ted twirled his eyeglasses by the earpiece. Once, he pointed at Daisy Mae's haunches, then left his stool to touch her fur. When she didn't wake, he pushed his hand deeper into the fur and petted her. Hezekiah tiptoed away softly as he'd come. Later, when he remembered again to visit his bears, he found Daisy Mae lapping water from the cage's tank, and Rosa and Ted were gone.

History Class

THE RESERVATION COMPUTER AT THE LOBBY DESK OF THE OLD
Farmington Inn has forgotten him, and he can't find his confirmation
number in his briefcase. Where are his reading glasses? "My wife's the
organized one," he explains. He squints into a pocket of his luggage.
The light's too dim, part of the inn's nineteenth-century decor: imitation gas lamps, paneling darkened as if by wood smoke, hardcover
editions of Hawthorne and Webster on the shelves, and a big-faced
innkeeper whose lips work the stem of a lit pipe as he fingers his own
drugstore glasses from a vest pocket and hands them across the counter. The lenses are smudged and scratched but magnify well enough.

After signatures and keys he settles into his room, charges the cell
phone (too late to call Rosa and the kids), slaps his face with icy water
from the bathroom faucet, unpacks. He checks inside a folder, assur-
ing himself once more that he remembered everything. Antique circus tickets sealed in a clear plastic bag. A photograph of his mother
that shows the scar on her face. A shoelace singed brown, also in plastic. A sixty-year-old headline, laminated on yellowed newsprint, that
reads, "Circus Blaze Kills Hundreds." Copies of e-mails he's exchanged
with a high-school sophomore named Lydia who first wrote: "I am
working on an honors history project about the Hartford Circus Fire
and I understand from newspaper articles that you are one of the last
living survivors . . ."

Outside, a dog barks, then barks again, and somewhere a chime is agitated to a jangle by the wind. He had wanted to lodge in Hartford, but this place is more pleasant than any he could find in the city. A quiet country inn for a quiet country town, which he remembers as full of apple orchards and money. The New England of Mr. Currier and Mr. Ives, and the room looks it. A four-poster bed. A checkerboard table. A framed print of tall ships in Hartford's long-vanished Dutch Point harbor. He grew up with a different Dutch Point, one where retired Italian men took fishing poles and coffee tins of worms or corn kernels on weekday mornings, the motors of their small boats leaking oil into the Connecticut River. Hartford, not *New England*. But he's here to visit both. Tomorrow, the city: Lydia and her history class, then his parents' graves. Rosa arrives Wednesday from North Carolina, and the next day they'll begin their autumn leaf tour of Massachusetts and Vermont. He returns to Hartford every few years, can't seem to stay away, and Rosa has visited with him for a funeral and for a birthday a few years back, but she's never seen the New England where farmers stain their barns red and innkeepers wear Abe Lincoln beards.

In bed, with a room-service tumbler of scotch brought by the innkeeper ("One day at a time myself," the innkeeper said, "expecting miracles"), he braces on stiff pillows and rereads Lydia's most recent e-mail to review the details. "Turn left," she wrote, "after you pass through the metal detector." Back home, as he headed for the door with luggage in hand, Rosa pinched his cheek and needled him for having a crush on the girl. "If she's tall and sexy, you run fast as you can," Rosa said. He wanted not to blush but did, because it's true: Lydia has charmed him. The formal tone of her notes, her address of him as "Mr. Theodore Liszak of North Carolina," the precision of her questions, the easy and excessive use of exclamation points to thank him for his answers. The invitation to visit her class flatters him, because it has been years since anyone—even his own children—showed interest in his dramatic history, but it troubles him, too, because he knows how little he has to say.

He was three years old. His mother brought him to a circus matinee. The tent ignited, then burned, and the fire peeled his flesh from ankle to collarbone.

He remembers none of it. He has never remembered. In his mind, he was born with the scars that crisscross his body. "It's a blessing that you don't remember," his mother used to say. For years he believed her and never pushed for more than the spare details she offered, settling instead for glimpses he dreamed that vanished as he woke.

One weekend afternoon in North Carolina, by the swimming pool, his own children asked about the fire. He'd forgotten his sunglasses indoors, so he lay on his stomach on a towel on the warm deck, beads of water sliding off him, his eyes closed and hot from the chlorine. He felt little hands on his skin, pressing, poking. Little breaths. Little gasps. He pretended to sleep until they shook him awake. They asked, and he answered, a conversation that he hoped could last forever but ended after a few minutes with a shoulder shrug. "I don't remember," he'd said, too many times. Then Ryan and Amber hurried off as if they'd only come for permission to color with crayons. He watched them go, squinting against the sunlight that glared off the water's surface, off the whiteness of the deck, off the metal flashing on the house's roof, all so blinding he had the sense that the light had erased him.

At breakfast, he watches an English setter gambol about the yard, a soggy rope in its mouth, bits of leaves tangled in the fringe of its tail. Beyond the dog lie gardens with mums still blooming autumn's colors, but the vegetable plants have frosted black. He sponges runny yolk into a piece of soft bread, and memory interrupts, surprising him with Lanie Chaponis who in second grade saw how the fire had marked him and who wouldn't put her fingers in the finger paint after he had touched it. And who, years later, in high school, opened her blouse and let his hands follow the curves of her breasts, and who kissed his scars hungrily. But another teenage girl intrudes on the memory, a live one carrying a coffeepot, asking about a refill.

A few hours later, past the metal detector, past a perfumed security guard whose upper arms are thick as fire hydrants, he arrives at the school office. "Lydia Turner," he says and learns that she has missed school today. Nevertheless, arrangements are made, and in the classroom the teacher tells him the story of an after-school fight. The other girl, troubled, used a knife. Lydia's wounds required surgery. She's home now from the hospital, but the teacher doesn't know when she'll come back to school. Maybe a week, maybe two. Maybe never. "Students sometimes vanish, yes," he says. "Change districts. Move back to the West Indies or New Haven, wherever they're from."

The teacher offers him a chair near the front, a place to wait until it's time to talk about the fire. The chair, made for a younger, more pliable body, pinches skin on his right hip. The teacher orders a girl in the back row to put away her headphones.

He remembers that in high school a nun once pointed to his scars and told him that God marks little boys for the wickedness He finds in their souls. Every boy in this classroom wears sneakers that look like carnival rides. Some girls do, too. The carpet is stained and littered with gum wrappers and paper bits sloughed from spiral notebooks. The ventilation system wheezes. Near the back a fat boy in a football jersey rests his forehead on the desk. The teacher reviews the history of school desegregation. "Topeka, Kansas," answers one student. "Little Rock Central," says another. "Sheff v. O'Neill," gargles a neatly dressed girl who sounds ill with pneumonia and barely holds her eyes open. The teacher's name, he sees, is written on the whiteboard, and he hopes a student will say the name so he learns how to pronounce it.

"Lydia's guest," announces the teacher, "survived Hartford's great circus fire. I wish she were here to introduce him, and I hope you all keep her in mind, and pray for her, and yourselves avoid violence. We must walk other paths, yes? Walk away from foolish trouble with our heads high. Walk away, yes. Walk away. Lydia began studying the Hartford circus fire for her honors project at the start of the school year. Yes, it is an important part of Hartford's history and as bad as it sounds. A circus tent burned with a crowd of women and children inside. Lydia's guest was a little boy at the circus that day. She has written him e-mails, yes, and he's come from North Carolina to share his experience with us."

Another nun had proclaimed him God's miracle, said that a guardian angel walked into the flames to rescue him, as Lord Jesus will one day stride through infernal perdition to free all sinners. "Dear Mr. Theodore Liszak of North Carolina," Lydia wrote. "Please if you come to Hartford . . ." He imagines the other girl's knife cutting into soft belly. The teacher, near the back of the room, makes violent, surreptitious hand signals to the fat boy in the football jersey, and the boy sits straight. The teacher wears a tie. Gold paisley.

Back home, he had decided against a tie because he thought the students might find it stuffy. Now, standing before this array of faces that show no hint of anticipation, his hand rises to his collar and he fiddles with the spot where a knot should be.

"High-school buddies called me Lizard Liszak," he says.

Lydia had declared the nickname "most interesting!!!!!" but the faces of her classmates remain static. No one even coughs. He says, "I'll explain why later."

Because it is easiest, he begins with facts: July 6, 1944. No known cause, no arsonist ever arrested. Fire rushed up a wall of the tent across the top and down the other side. The band's musicians blew their horns until smoke scalded their lungs. Women died. Children died. More than one hundred fifty people. But no animal suffered, not a whisker singed.

"It was near here, a couple miles to the east. On Barbour Street."

Then his story: How his mother brought him to the circus that day. How his father was absent, off to fight the Nazis in Italy. The weeks he lay in the hospital, the surgeries to patch his skin. The scar his mother carried on her face throughout her life.

He remembers the photograph and passes it to a girl in front. She looks a moment, hands it to a girl behind her.

His own scars. He bunches up his sleeves to show them. "Lizard Liszak," he says. But the football boy's head is again flat on the desk. The pretty girl who gargles her words fishes in her purse. He looks at his arms and sees what they see: aged flesh. The fire's markings, old friends to him and in his youth a startling sight, look less exotic set against coffee-stained teeth and liver spots and sagging, withering skin. He notices a boy with his own scar, pencil-thin and running the length of his forearm.

"I don't remember the fire," he says. "I was three years old. But I have read about it, and people who were older told me stories. They said they'd never forget that day."

The boy with the forearm scar gives back the photograph.

"Oh! and I have the actual circus tickets. And this is a shoelace I wore that day."

The souvenirs make their way around the room. Students shift in their seats, glance at their cell phone screens. The teacher prompts them for questions. Finally a boy asks, "Do you know Alonzo Smith? He's my uncle, and he lives in North Carolina," and the students laugh.

On display at the front of the room, the scarred relic smiles through his failure. When the laughter quiets, he asks, "Which desk belongs to Lydia?" and a few students point. The empty seat holds a place in the middle, shading to the room's left, between a boy with handcuffs on his backpack and a girl with fingernails long and curled and painted pink, white, and orange.

"How is she?"

The students ignore the question. Instead each looks elsewhere: at a notebook, at a dropped comb on the rug. The boy with the scar pinches the wound along his arm.

"Please," he says.

A few students turn to the teacher, who nods permission.

"Not good," answers one.

"She got cut bad."

"Girl who did it's in jail."

He asks what started the fight. Too many voices answer, then grow louder, and he can't make out anything through the din. The teacher quiets them, then picks one.

"Her brother got in a fight with this other girl's brother and beat him pretty bad. So this other girl wanted payback."

His hand worries the absent knot once more. The students wait for another question. God, they're so beautiful, and he fears his eyes might tear. The bell saves him. Smiling students politely return the tokens of his one-time troubles, which now seem to him old beyond reason and foolish. After Alonzo Smith's nephew apologizes to him at the teacher's insistence, he asks the teacher about Lydia. He wants to visit. Is there an address? "Maybe at the office," the teacher says. But no, the woman at the counter won't release students' records. Privacy laws. Perhaps he'd like to send a get-well card in care of the school that they might forward to her? Yes, he'll do that. "And do you have a phone book?" He looks up her last name, Turner, finds too many to call. On the way out he waves to the security guard with arms like fire hydrants. "Thanks for visiting," she says.

He wonders if the wounds are in her shoulder or her stomach or if she's slashed along the palms of her hands. He wonders whether her gashes have been stapled or glued or stitched.

He drives streets near the school, as if he might discover her on a sidewalk—though he wouldn't know her to see her—and he studies each teenaged girl who plays hooky, looking for one who is hurt, on crutches or in a wheelchair or bandaged. He searches for the name *Turner* on mailboxes. He drives until he's driven roads all over Hartford's North End, until he parks at the spot on Barbour Street where he and his mother came that day to see clowns and prancing ponies. Now it is an elementary school named for a man called Wish. Nearby, a fellow in a hooded sweatshirt taps out an open-palmed rhythm on an upturned garbage can and sings; a gray-haired woman passes by carrying plastic grocery bags overflowing with purple plastic flowers. For a moment he thinks to leave his car, to walk the grounds and hallways of the school and discover whether there is a plaque, some memorial for the dead. But he pictures himself as class lets out, standing in front of such a plaque with scores of children dodging his legs. They'd hurry past, forgetting already how to add fractions or what is the capital of Egypt, ignoring him and that plaque: two throwbacks, obvious and invisible. Imagining all this, he drives on.

★ ★ ★

At the cemetery, he guides the sedan at a crawl beneath a canopy of leaves brushed gold and red. Marble monuments and tombs. A pyramid in rosy marble. A rifle carved from granite. Grassy mounds seasoned with fallen leaves. He touches a button and lowers the window on his side. He prefers autumn weather. "Yankee," his wife has always accused. But she knows why summer troubles him, that season when his mother made him wear long pants and long-sleeved shirts no matter how blistering the day, so he wouldn't be teased about his scars. He had never minded being teased.

He parks at a place he guesses is near his parents' graves. A decade later, and this part of the cemetery still feels young. Here the names are eastern European and Italian, the memorials plain, designed for the working class. His father wanted a ground plate, his mother an upright stone. She won the argument by dying first; Papa could never deny her. He searches for their marker, passing as he does a fresh grave, dirt mounded and damp, crosses himself, not out of piety or his Roman Catholic habits, but out of some deeper hope.

When he finds Papa and Mama, he squats and with a toothpick from his shirt pocket pokes crud out of the *L* and the *Z*. Too many years since his last visit, and their place looks lonely and cold, without flowers, without the warmth that comes with familiarity. He tosses the toothpick aside and promises to visit more often, tomorrow and again the day Rosa arrives. A gust lifts leaves and tosses them around his feet. He thinks of the students handling his mother's photograph, her likeness passed from hand to hand and tucked now in a folder in his briefcase, between a headline and a shoelace. Mama always let Papa trace the scar on her face with the tip of his index finger. Papa blew smoke rings from a cigar and put polka records on the hi-fi, and Mama danced. Mama always danced.

He sits in the grass and rests against the cold stone, and remembers a day when he was nine. She had run away. This was nothing new. She ran away often. Each time she returned with a gift and a story: a mica-filled rock she said was chipped from a star, a rabbit's foot that had belonged to Peter Cottontail's unlucky cousin, a goblet from King Arthur's table, a fork FDR had used to eat meatloaf. Thank you, he said, and buried the trinkets beneath clothes in his dresser drawers. He didn't want to keep them, but he couldn't throw them away, either.

During this time when he was nine, an early autumn as temperate as today, she had been gone nearly a week. Only his father's manner kept him from panic: Papa's careful raking of leaves in the backyard; the way Papa tucked him into bed at night, blankets tight around the edges of his body so that he felt wrapped like King Tut. On the fifth day, Papa taught him chess. At the backyard picnic table, Papa lit a cigarette, opened a beer. For the boy, a straw in a cold bottle of ginger ale. He lifted his father's cigarette lighter, sniffed the tang of its butane.

Papa named the pieces. He explained the pawns and knights and was about to start on bishops when Mama appeared. She smiled her beautiful Jennifer Jones movie-star smile, and she kissed her son on the head, and sat beside him on the picnic bench. His mother said nothing, and neither did his father. He kept quiet, too, because he knew if he spoke, he would cry.

Papa kept on. He spoke of the bishops and the rooks, and then the queen, who was the most powerful. The queen goes anywhere, he said, as far as she wants. Then there is the king. The king is not powerful at all but is the reason for the game. "No piece," he said, "is more valuable than the king."

When they began a practice game, Mama left for the house. Through an open window, he heard her draw a bath.

His father guided him through the game, saving him from checkmate by saying, "Good enough for today. Go to Franklin Avenue," and his father handed over two dollar bills. "Get pastries for dessert."

He pretended to leave as his father had ordered, but instead hid inside the bosom of a neighbor's giant rhododendron, then crept back beneath the open bathroom window and crouched against the cold concrete of the foundation.

"Don't look at me that way!" he heard his mother say.

"I thought this time you might not come back," said his father.

"I was starving. Mice ate my knapsack and all my rye bread."

His mother laughed, and his father said nothing. He pictured Papa standing in the doorway, then crossing to the toilet and sitting on the lid. He pictured Mama reaching with a soapy, wet hand to touch his father's suspenders.

Mama said, "I want you to miss me."

What his father said next, he couldn't hear. Then Mama said, "I want you to miss me, and I want you to wonder about me. You must not forget me."

"How could I forget you?" his father asked.

"You could," said his mother. "You would want to."

"You will ruin me," his father said.

"I might," she said, and her voice quavered. "I am a powerful queen."

Huddled outside the window, he listened, oddly sad and comforted. When he grew older, he would wonder why his mother thought it more important to be remembered than to be kind. But then, when he was nine, he promised himself that for her sake he would never forget her. On Franklin Avenue, he bought raspberry tarts.

And now? He loses more of her every day. Already he cannot recall what she wore that afternoon of chess and cigarettes and tub water, and he can't say for the life of him the color of her eyes. He can't even remember how she looked on the day she was buried. He remembers a fact: Her hair was tangled. He remembers a fact: He once bought raspberry tarts. He remembers a fact: Long ago he boarded a bus on a summer morning, wanting—and not realizing he wanted—to live where people had never heard the story of his circus afternoon. He thinks of Lydia Turner's classroom again, and of Topeka, Kansas, and Little Rock Central, and he knows such facts are distant and without temperature. Closer is that raw grave, and somewhere, at some address still denied him, a girl with cuts in her flesh. A warm breeze touches the soft skin between his collarbones, and beneath his boots as he walks: the gentle shush of leaves.

★ ★ ★

At the inn that night he asks for a telephone book. Under the Hartford listings he finds Lydia's teacher, who answers the ring.

"Leviticus. I think that's her father's name. Leviticus Turner. From Belize or Honduras. I can't recall."

Under the Ts, Leviticus Turner on Capen Street. A phone number and a street address. Apartment 2C. But when he calls, he hears a message that the line has been disconnected.

He telephones home, tells Ryan and Amber about his visit to the cemetery. Ryan says "okay," then asks whether he can drive the SUV while Mom and Dad are up north; Amber asks for intervention with Mom who won't let her stay overnight at a boy's house ("But he's gay, Dad!"). When Rosa takes the phone, he mentions the stabbing. "I don't know why the line is disconnected," he says, "but I'll drive by tomorrow." She reminds him to bring a gift, something he can return if he doesn't find the girl, and again he feels grateful for his wife.

Later, in bathrobe and socks, he looks at his mother's photograph, but the photo is black-and-white after all, so no, it won't tell him the color of her eyes.

★ ★ ★

Most apartment buildings on that block of Capen Street look empty and lack address numbers, so he asks the lavender stuffed puppy in the passenger seat what he should do. At the door of his best guess, a boy's voice sounds from the intercom in answer to his ring. He explains who he is, the e-mails, the invitation to class. "She's asleep now, but come up," says the boy, and the door buzzes.

The long hallway smells of cat urine and fried food. The boy who opens the door at 2C looks about fifteen. His Orlando Magic jersey is mended and too large for him. He's barefoot and in shorts that fall past his kneecaps, and his hair is neat. The apartment is tidy and almost empty, with a red couch, a table and some chairs, and a boxy acoustic guitar in one corner. The only mess is a small one on the table, where packets of sugar and ketchup lie, torn open and shaken and squeezed empty. The curtains are drawn and glowing with sunlight.

"She'll like the dog," the boy says as they shake hands. His lilt sounds musical, full of sea spray and sand. As he speaks he turns his attention again and again to the room where his sister must lie asleep. "She talked about you. From North Carolina." The boy pronounces the state as if the sound tickles him. The boy's name, he learns, is George. The older brother.

"Have to wake her soon to change her bandages. Maybe she'll talk to you then."

Shy to ask more questions, he stays quiet. He's not her teacher or a doctor, not a family friend. A radiator against the wall bangs twice.

George says, "I hate them that did this. Father says no, don't hate. The other girl's just a girl. But I hate that girl. I'd kill her if I saw her. Don't make it worse, man. That's what Father says. So it's good I stay home with Lydia, you see? By her side 24/7, you know? Take care of her *and* keep myself from doing the thing I'd regret."

From Lydia's room comes a whimper, and George goes to her.

Behind at the table, he listens to their quiet talk, the language something like English but more melodious, and a few words he understands. Outside, something shades the sun, and the puppy looks less purple in the clouded light.

". . . won't see nobody. Tell him . . . go please."

That young voice, loud with strength and defeat, and he bites the inside of his cheek. George executes his duty, apologizes, receives the purple puppy on Lydia's behalf.

In the hallway he shuts his eyes, listens, but another voice, a stranger's, shouts from outside, and even through the door and walls it quiets the memory of her voice to a breeze. The carpet, he notices, is worn in places to the plastic webbing underneath. "You must not forget me," his mother had ordered, and he promised only to learn too late how cruel she was to ask the impossible, to extract a promise he'd fail to keep no matter how much he loved her. He would rather be kind. He would rather memory be ruined as everything else is ruined. The purple puppy was no kindness if it reminds her. Better to have stayed away.

★ ★ ★

"Have you heard of the circus fire?"

The innkeeper nods, speaks of how Emmett Kelly the famous clown once stayed at the inn, the stories he told. The men bookend the hearth. The innkeeper charges his pipe, and the tobacco smells of nutmeg. A pair of other guests play a word game on a board. Wind batters the windows, gasps as it forces its way through eaves and around the edges of doors. In his glass of scotch, the ice melts quickly. He sips before he begins.

"The Greatest Show on Earth," he says, hocus-pocus words to evoke a memory he doesn't have. "Inside the tent smelled pungent. Animals and perfume and sweat. My mother and I sat in the bleachers near the band." He tells the innkeeper which marches the band played. Then he describes aerialists, jugglers, dancing bears. The fire surprised us all, he says, swept like wind across the tent, an apocalyptic fury from horizon to horizon, a blanket of flame draped over the sky. And as he creates the scene for the innkeeper, imagining the singed mane of a lion, the garlic breath of a clown, the bleeding mascara of a skirted girl, he finds himself younger, trapped in the tent. His mother screams, grown-ups push and yank at each other, stumbling, and their panic frightens him. He can't run, can't avoid the knees and footfalls of people who think of nothing but their own survival. Where is his mother? He yells for her, but the flames make such awful noise. He falls and bumps his head. He stands and loses balance, and suddenly he's toppling off the bleachers, falling through air, a little boy in summer shorts and shoes with laces knotted twice, plummeting through heat and the rush of air, too young even to imagine that there is something called death. On the ground his body won't work anymore. Bits of straw tickle his nose. He can't move. Heat like the most savage cold weighs on him, and the weight eats away his clothes, invades his skin and the skin under his skin. What's worse is the fear, his trembling heart, the emerging awareness that his mother is not the world, and that the world hates him.

The innkeeper looks gut-shot, staring at the hearth fire. "Is that what you told the kids at the school?"

The scotch tastes too much like ash. He sets the glass on a lace doily on a side table. "No," he says, satisfied that he'll tell no one else ever again.

The next day he wakes to quiet rain and sits at the window of his room for half an hour watching it fall. Later, sweatered, he sits in a rocking chair on the porch and reads Hawthorne. After lunch he skims the newspaper and discovers that there's a soccer game that afternoon between Farmington's boys and Glastonbury's. When the rain lets up he drives to the high school and watches the teams compete. Then he's off to meet Rosa's plane.

The airport donuts taste stale, but he hurries one down. Rosa comes to him from behind glass doors, eyes bloodshot from travel and not so vivid a green, but she's laughing and telling of a conversation she overheard on the plane between two young women who had piercings, and the confession of the one who wore a ring through her clitoris. "No," she'd giggled to the other, "it's even *better.*" From there to dinner at what was once a gristmill in Manchester, then back to the inn where they keep each other up late in the warm bed. The next morning at breakfast, their table is a collage of maps and tourist brochures and sections of the morning paper. Rosa asks whether he'd like to visit his parents' graves one last time before leaving Hartford, and he shakes his head, he's paid his respects, so she leans over a section of the newspaper and, after a minute or two, reads to him a story about parents in Ohio who want teachers to give their children more homework.

Acknowledgments

THANKS TO JOHN REIMRINGER AND KATRINA VANDENBERG, WHO loved each page as if it were their own. Thanks also to the many writers who have read these stories and offered keen insights, especially those at the University of Arkansas and the Sewanee Writers' Conference. Great institutions are so because of their people.

I'm grateful to Michael Griffith, editor of the Yellow Shoe Fiction series, for choosing this book and for his careful attention to its sentences. Thanks, too, to the talented, dedicated people with LSU Press, the best friends a book can have.

A grant from the National Endowment for the Arts helped make this book possible.

For my understanding of the circus fire, I'm indebted to Lynne Tuohy, who inspired me with her reporting for the *Hartford Courant* nearly fifty years after the event; and to Stewart O'Nan, whose nonfiction book *The Circus Fire* remains as thorough a piece of historical journalism as I've ever read.

Thanks to Esmond Harmsworth for having faith, and to the journal editors who also believed, especially Robert Stewart at *New Letters*, Megan Sexton and Sheri Joseph at *Five Points*, and Stephen Corey at the *Georgia Review*.

And here's to the ringmasters: Donald "Skip" Hays, John Duval, William Harrison, Joanne Meschery, and the late James Whitehead.

My greatest love and appreciation goes to Sheri Venema, who walked with me into the tent and stayed for the whole show.